Royal
REBEL

I start changing into my **DUNGAREES**, **SUNGLASSES**, **PINK WIG** and **TIARA**. Once I'm ready I look into the large gold-framed mirror leaning against the wall and smile.

I am **TIARA GIRL**.

I am a **ROYAL REBEL!**

To my readers, this one is for you...
Always follow your heart – and remember:
there is a queen in every one of us!
Royally yours,
Carina xx
In loving memory of the real Alice.

First published in the UK in 2019 by Usborne Publishing Ltd.,
Usborne House, 83-85 Saffron Hill, London EC1N 8RT, England.

www.usborne.com

Copyright © Carina Axelsson, 2019

Cover photo: Source Models/photography by Tiffany Mumford

Cover and illustrations copyright © Usborne Publishing Ltd, 2019

Author photo © Carina Axelsson, 2019

The right of Carina Axelsson to be identified as the author of this work has
been asserted by her in accordance with the Copyright, Designs and
Patents Act, 1988.

The name Usborne and the devices ♀ ⊕ are Trade Marks of
Usborne Publishing Ltd.

A CIP catalogue record for this book is available from the British Library.

ISBN 9781474942409 JFMAMJJASON /18 04767-3

Printed in the UK.

Royal REBEL

CARINA AXELSSON

USBORNE

Chapter ONE

7.01 a.m., Monday, at the palace

Hi Tiara Girl! And welcome to your channel!

Your most recent video:

Tiara Girl's Top Three Back-to-School
Hairstyles has had:

150 views

WHAT? I lean in close to my laptop and peer carefully at the small black numbers.

150 views…

I stare for a moment more, then rub my eyes. Late last night there were only eight views…I'm sure.

I pull my pyjama sleeve down over my wrist and use it to wipe at the screen, but the number doesn't change. So, no, it definitely isn't smudged chocolate. I pull back with a sharp intake of breath.

Maybe it's a mistake?

Maybe something is wrong with my computer?

After all, I've never had a video go beyond twenty views before.

I reload the page and what I see makes me jump back from my computer and bring my hands to my mouth in disbelief.

210 views…

HUH? Sixty more people have just watched my video in the time I've been staring at the screen!

Okay…this is no joke. My latest Tiara Girl video is already getting **WAY** more views than my three previous videos put together!

I only filmed the video yesterday afternoon, on my phone. I propped the phone up on some books and talked my way through three different hairstyles: a high sleek ponytail, a half-up/half-down style with a couple of cute hair clips and an amazing French braid that went front to back but then wrapped round the head.

Coco, my cocker spaniel, is in the video too, and I even braided her brown topknot (it is pretty long). So I guess that's actually four hairstyles, although Coco's doesn't really count because she's not going back to school. But she did look really cute! I put some pink-gold glitter around my eyes and we wore matching pink tops (both of which I made myself). Then I added some stars and captions to the video before uploading it late last night.

One word:

LOVE!

Of course I might be a tiny bit biased...but seriously, I dare you to watch it and not agree that it's the cutest thing ever.

And now over two hundred people have seen the video!

I stand up, throw my fists in the air and dance in a circle before leaping onto my bed. I start bouncing up and down, singing at the top of my lungs. Coco, after a moment's confusion, picks up on my excitement, leaps onto the bed and shimmies and barks beside me, her tail wagging happily.

"I'm a vlogger! A real, live vlogger!" I laugh as I spring up and down. "Tiara Girl, I love you!"

I tell myself I'll become the best, most amazing and totally awesome fashion vlogger anyone has ever seen! Nothing will stop me. **NOTHING!!!**

At that moment I hear a knock on my bedroom door, followed by a clipped voice. "Your Royal Highness? Time to get ready for school. You're expected at breakfast in twenty minutes."

All the excitement suddenly zaps out of me and I fall onto my rumpled sheets like a limp balloon. Coco licks my face as I sigh.

Ugh! *That!* And just when I'd forgotten…

That is the one small detail that might possibly

stand between me and my whole fashion-vlogging dream.

Personally, I could work around it. I mean, *I* don't think it's *that* big a deal...

Okay, maybe it is... I guess it depends how you look at it.

Anyway...what I forgot to mention is that...er... umm...I'm a princess.

Yeah, I know, it adds a twist.

And you're probably asking yourself, what's the problem? A princess can do whatever she wants, right?

Wrong.

On its own, being a princess wouldn't be such a problem if it wasn't for one other little detail... I'm also first in line to the throne of the Queendom of Waldenburg.

Yup, that small fairy-tale-like queendom high in the mountains between France and Germany. Well, I'm its princess and my mum is its queen.

And according to my mum (Her Majesty Sophia XII, Queen of Waldenburg, if you want to be technical), if there is *one* thing (actually, according to my mother there are many, but for the sake of simplicity I'll stick to one here) a princess and future queen does *not* do, it's vlog about fashion...

So if my situation sounds tricky, that's because it is.

And guess what? I think it's about to become a lot trickier...

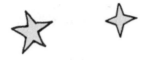

Chapter TWO

7.30 a.m., still in my bedroom

Okay, I bet you're dying to ask me a bunch of princess questions. I know this because almost everyone I meet asks me what it's like to be a princess and live in a palace.

I'm always a bit tongue-tied when asked though, because for me it's my normal life. Like, I don't know anything other than being a princess... Having said that, I know I'm lucky to live in such a beautiful house...er, palace...with my mum and dad and grandmother. And Coco, Cupcake (my pony), and Zoë (my guinea pig).

So what's the palace like?

Hmm...I guess the best way to answer is with a list.

I like to write lists. I may as well let you know this now because you're going to come across a lot of them. So here's the first one...

FIVE THINGS YOU SHOULD KNOW ABOUT WALDENBURG PALACE:

1. It's set on a chunk of rock jutting out from a high mountain. And the castle has lots and lots of towers and turrets – so, yeah, it looks really dreamy.

2. Oodles and oodles of people work at the palace. There are footmen and cooks, cleaners, housekeepers, butlers, drivers, ladies-in-waiting, gardeners, security guards, soldiers, a grand chamberlain, and even a press office. I would have to write a whole new list in order to include them all. Basically, if you live in a palace, don't expect to ever be alone.

3. Also, I'm not exactly sure how many rooms

there are in the palace but I remember Grandmaman once said it was over eight hundred. Some of them, like the Guards Gallery, are large enough that, if she wanted to, Mum could have a tennis court and stadium benches put in. Others are just big enough for a tiny sofa and table – what Grandmaman calls a boudoir. She says that hundreds of years ago my great-great-great-great- (I'm not sure how many greats) grandmother Adelaide created the tiny light green and gold boudoir and made it big enough for only one person – herself – so that she could have some peace and quiet. Today Grandmaman likes to sit in the boudoir while she solves her sudoku puzzles.

4. The most impractical thing about living in a palace is the distance you have to walk to get anywhere. For example: a midnight snack. The palace kitchen is still in the cellar (as it has been since 1580), so getting a snack is no easy thing, trust me. It takes me something like fifteen minutes **(ONE WAY!)** to walk from my

bedroom on the second floor of the Renaissance wing, to the kitchen in the cellar of the west wing. When you live in a palace you really have to try hard not to forget anything when you leave your bedroom because it might take you half an hour just to go back and fetch it.

5. The palace has a ghost and his name is Eberhart. He's a German count who married a Waldenburg queen four hundred years ago. Legend has it he married her in the hope of taking the queendom from her, but when his plan was discovered the Queen's Mountain Guard cornered him on the battlements of one of the castle's many towers and pushed him into the ravine far below. People sometimes see his ghost as it runs along the battlements (spooky!). It is said he is waiting to avenge his death and will one day strike down a Waldenburg queen. As Crown Princess I can't say that this makes me very enthusiastic about sitting on the throne.

Anyway time to get ready for breakfast.

After jumping off my bed I hurriedly dress in my school uniform: navy and green tartan skirt, white blouse, maroon tie and navy blazer. If you asked a psychologist, she'd probably say that my need to vlog about fashion stems from my school uniform. Not that I dislike it, but…it's a *uniform*. And it's not even a nice one. Is it any wonder I have to spend my free time expressing my own personal style?

I quickly message my BFF Leonie Leonberger about my super-exciting Tiara Girl viewer numbers. As I'm texting, Sandra (who used to be my nanny and now looks after my clothes and helps me pack my suitcase when I travel and stuff), comes in to ask me if I need any help. What Sandra really means, though, is *Let me have a look at you and make sure you look like a princess before you step out of the palace.* Sandra likes things just so. Even if I am only going to school.

I put a clip in my hair and assure Sandra everything is under control, while checking that Zoë has enough fresh water in her cage. Then I run from my bedroom to the middle of the baroque wing downstairs (by running I can do it in five minutes instead of twelve) with Sandra following behind at a brisk walk.

I meet about five maids along the way and even though I've told them they don't need to curtsy to me, they still do. "You will be a queen one day, Princess Lily, so you can begin getting used to it now," Sandra says with a smile, as she catches up with me in the ballroom. I'm scuffling with Coco to get the tennis ball out of her mouth – she's carried it all the way from my bedroom.

Yes, there is a ballroom in the palace, and, yes, if you saw it, it would remind you of *Beauty and the Beast*. It's long, two storeys high, and white, with lots of glittering gold plasterwork. The ceiling is painted with pink cherubs and a hazy blue sky. Enormous mirrors line one side of it and large windows the other. There are two huge fireplaces at either end of the room and crystal chandeliers hang in two lines along the ceiling. The only thing missing is the handsome prince. Ha ha! That was a joke: in Waldenburg we only have princesses!

I finally get the ball away from Coco and raise my arm to throw it.

"You really shouldn't be playing with balls in here, Your Royal Highness, if I may say so."

"But why not?"

I briefly wonder if all thirteen year olds have someone telling them what to do all the time. Or am I the only one? Because sometimes – like now – it really *feels* like I'm the only one.

"Because you might hit someone, or something, accidentally."

"But who besides us is going to be in the ballroom at eight in the morning?" I laugh and stand in front of Sandra, then throw the ball backwards over my head. By the time I see Sandra's eyes widen in horror, it's too late. I turn just in time to watch the ball bounce off the forehead of our Court Master of Ceremonies.

And now he has a big red mark there.

I apologize but he's amused. Still, Sandra can't resist saying, "I told you so, Princess Lily," as we step out of the ballroom.

She has a point, so I don't say anything, and run

down the corridor instead as Sandra waves goodbye.

Finally, I reach the small dining room (there are three dining rooms in the palace – the small one is the one we use when it's just us) and open the door. There I find my grandmother speaking to Alice (aka Alice Victoria, Countess of Vendelstein, Mistress of the Robes to the Royal Court of Waldenburg).

"Good morning, Grandmaman!" I say as I rush in, Coco at my heels.

I come in so quickly that I catch the footman standing outside the dining room by surprise. I hear him jump behind me, too late to stop the door from slamming shut. My grandmother and Alice wince at the noise.

"Sorry!" I say.

"Lily, if I've told you once, I've told you a thousand times, a princess does not rush – anywhere."

"But I'm late!"

"Precisely my point, my dear," Grandmaman answers as she turns her face up for me to kiss. "A princess never rushes because a princess is *never* late. And she's especially never late because she's been throwing balls for her dog in the ballroom."

WHAT? How come Grandmaman always knows everything?

She is wearing a lilac dress, with matching coat and hat. A large multi-gemstone brooch on her swishy coat and sapphires at her ears provide a dazzling touch of colour. I can smell her rose scent as I lean in. "Punctuality is the politeness of queens," she reminds me. "Now, say good morning to Alice."

Have I mentioned that Grandmaman always has to have the last word? I tell you, the whole princess thing is only easy in the movies.

Alice has been my mother's Mistress of the Robes since before I was born, and before that she was my grandmother's Mistress of the Robes. So that tells you how long she's been around. Earlier in her career she was also a general with the Waldenburg army, so she's a stickler for protocol – at times she even corrects Grandmaman.

Which is why Alice has been handpicked by my mother to teach me all about my future role as Queen of Waldenburg. Of course, I learn a lot from my mum and grandmother. But because Mum is so busy running the queendom and because Grandmaman still keeps a pretty packed official schedule (despite having abdicated – **FYI**: that's basically a fancy word that queens and kings use instead of "retirement" – in favour of my mum), Alice steps in regularly.

In fact, starting today, after school, Alice will be teaching me everything about being a Crown Princess and Queen-to-be in my new Princess Class. I'm starting Princess Class because on my fourteenth birthday (which is about six months away) I will "come of age", as Grandmaman puts it. This means that from the day I turn fourteen I will officially begin my royal duties. It's a Waldenburg royal tradition: every Crown Princess for the last nine hundred years has done the same. This makes it difficult (okay, impossible) to say, *Umm, actually, Mum and Dad, I don't really feel ready to start my royal duties just yet, do you mind if we wait until I'm sixteen?* I think the castle would crumble before *that* happened.

Of course, there's already a lot of princess stuff I know, like how to wave from the balcony of the palace and who I should curtsy to… So in fact my Princess Class will focus more on the Queen-to-be stuff, like how the Waldenburg government works, signing laws into existence, and Waldenburg foreign diplomacy.

Yeah, I know, it's not exactly what fairy tales are made of.

But I'm sure Princess Class will be okay. Besides, despite her frosty reputation, Alice is actually very nice. Really. Even if she can go on for hours about royal protocol.

THREE THINGS ALICE SAYS A PRINCESS MUST ALWAYS BE:

1. A princess must always be on time. She can be five minutes early, but never five minutes late.
2. A princess must always be friendly. Alice says people never forget the moment they meet a real-life princess, so if you smile and are friendly they'll always think well of you – and if you don't they'll always think ill of you. "But what if I'm just having a bad day?" I asked Alice once.

"Princesses never have bad days," she answered.

3. A princess must always dress well. Unfortunately for me, being well dressed is nowhere near the same as being fashionably dressed. Well dressed, says Alice, means looking appropriate for whatever royal function I'm expected to attend. So, for instance, I should know to wear a bright-coloured dress to the palace summer garden party, or Waldenburg traditional folk costume for Waldenburg National Day. Being fashionable (i.e. wearing my favourite customized jeans or a cool top), on the other hand is for fashion magazines. I once asked her what was so wrong with that. I thought she was going to faint before she straightened her already straight back, turned to me and said, "Fashion magazines are common! You on the other hand represent nine hundred years of Waldenburg history." Then she gave me a look that would make lemons seem sweet.

"Well, I really must go now, Lily. I have to open that new museum in the Mont Chermoix district," Grandmaman says as a footman pulls her chair out from behind her and she stands to leave. I kiss Grandmaman goodbye and only sit back down after she has left the room.

I hear a shuffling of papers as Alice places her reading glasses onto the tip of her nose and goes over her notes. As Mistress of the Robes, Alice's official role is to coordinate the schedules of my mother's ladies-in-waiting and see to it that my mother's wardrobe and jewellery are in order. She also sometimes accompanies my mother on her state visits and is present at all official Waldenburg events.

Because today is Monday, Alice is present during my breakfast to give me a rundown of the coming week's schedule. This will include anything that I might have to do, like answer letters from young Waldenburg citizens, or pose for a new official portrait. She'll also remind me of anything big my mum has going on, like trips and official events, especially if they're taking place in the palace – so I don't accidentally open the wrong door and surprise Mum while she's talking politics with the King of Bhutan, for example.

"Your mother and father are still away, so tonight you'll have plenty of time for homework. Plus, don't forget, we will have your first Princess Class later." Alice looks up. "Tomorrow, your parents will return from their state visit to Brazil. And on Friday evening your mother is hosting a reception for two dozen new ambassadors and their husbands and wives. Several of our ministers, and the Mayor of Waldenburg and her husband, will also attend." Alice pauses briefly and eyes me over her reading glasses. "Your mother called me this morning, Lily; she thinks you should join her for this event. She thinks it's time...and I agree."

I'm shocked. This is the first time my mum has asked me to attend a formal event of this level (I'm not counting the time I met the US President – I was only three after all, and in my bathrobe because I'd just had my bath).

I stare up at Alice as the reality of this new step sinks in. "On Friday evening the guests will convene at 7.15 p.m. in the Yellow Salon," she continues. "You will walk in together with the Master of Ceremonies at 7.28 p.m. *precisely*." Alice gives me a stern look. "And your mother, accompanied by me, will walk in at 7.30 p.m. Dinner is scheduled for 8 p.m. in the Tapestry Hall."

"And?" What I really want to know is the dress code. I wish Alice would skip all the details and just get to it. But despite the fact that she is Mistress of the **ROBES**, she's certainly taking her time!

"A list of all the guests' names and a programme of the evening's events will be waiting for you in your bedroom when you return from school today. I will also have brief biographies of every guest prepared for you. We'll go over them together at your Princess Class tonight. This is so that you will know—"

"—how to converse with them at dinner," I interrupt. "I know, I know, Alice! Now how about my clothes?"

Alice does not look amused. "You're too interested in clothes, Lily."

"But I have to look nice! This is my first super-formal event!"

"True, but being interested in the event and wanting to act appropriately for the occasion should be your first concern."

I wish I could be given a bag of glitter every time I hear the word *appropriate*. I stick my tongue out at Alice as she rattles off more details but fortunately she doesn't notice.

Finally she pauses and purses her lips. "Dress code is white tie, medals and tiaras."

"**YAY!**" I jump up and scream with excitement. "Tiaras! Please tell me I get to wear a tiara, Alice, **PLEASE**?" You see, despite the fact that my vlog is called *Tiara* Girl, and that I'm a princess...the truth is, I've never worn a tiara – I mean one with *real* sparkly gems. I've worn tons of DIY ones, because I love to make them...but they're not quite the same thing... Anyway, I think this totally excuses my **MEGA EXCITEMENT** at the fact that I might just finally get to wear a real one!!! Not that Alice is itching to talk about it.

"Do sit down, Lily." Alice purses her lips again as

she points to my chair. "Your mother has requested that you wear a new ballgown."

"Great! I have something I made that would be perfect." My super fluffy and sparkly purple tulle dress with silver sequins springs to mind but Alice has other ideas. (Tulle, by the way, is what tutus are made of. Yay!)

"In this instance, Lily, your mother and your grandmother have already chosen a ballgown for you."

I can't believe I finally get to wear a ballgown – but it's not going to be one I've made! "But—"

"No buts," Alice interrupts. "Sandra will take your new ballgown to your room later so that you can try it on. And for the first time you will also wear your Queen Sophia sash and medal."

"And?" I point to the top of my head.

Alice rolls her eyes – something she only does when it's just the two of us, in private. "Try to be serious, Lily."

"I am. Very. But you said tiara."

I watch as Alice shuffles her notes again. "And,

yes, for the first time, in preparation for your increased duties after your fourteenth birthday, you will wear a tiara... But it will be a small one – a *starter* tiara, if you will," Alice emphasizes.

But I don't care if it's the size of a hairgrip – I'm going to wear a tiara at a real event. Finally!

"Which one do I get to wear?" I ask as I hug Coco.

"Your mother will lend you the Queen Josephine Pink Diamond Tiara." (Royal Info: most tiaras have names. They're usually named after queens, or their stones, or style.)

I jump up and twirl around Alice while Coco barks. The Queen Josephine Pink Diamond Tiara! I know exactly which one it is – my mother showed it to me once and I've seen it in our private family photo albums (it's never been photographed by the press); it's the one she used to wear when she was my age. It's glittery and gorgeous and sprinkled with a hundred tiny pink diamonds. And I'm going to wear it on Friday night!

Suddenly a **GREAT** idea comes to me. Wouldn't it be super cool to do a vlog about wearing a tiara?

A **REAL** tiara? Something like: **Tiara Girl's Top Tips for Wearing a Tiara?**

I've included tiaras in almost all my videos – my vlog is called Tiara Girl after all – but they've been DIY ones...

* Vlog #1: **Tiara Girl's Top Tips for Making Matching Tiaras for You and Your Dog!**

* Vlog #2: **Get Your Pony Glitzed Out – Tiara Girl Style!** Okay, so strictly speaking, a halter is not a tiara, but because it was coated with glitter it did kind of look like one.

* Vlog #3: **Tiara Girl's DIY Matching Tiara and Tutu for You and Your Guinea Pig!**

* Vlog #4: **Tiara Girl's Top Three Back-To-School Hairstyles.** Ha! No tiara in this one, so all the more reason to include a **REAL** one now!

With that last thought in mind, and before Alice realizes that something's afoot, I head to the door. The last thing I need is Alice getting suspicious about anything concerning my vlog. It's a **SECRET** after all

– and that's how I intend to keep it. "Goodbye, Alice!" I say as I grab my school bag.

"We're not finished."

"But if we don't stop now I won't make it to school on time – and someone once told me that a princess should never be late!"

"Very well. We'll speak more when you're back."

"I'm riding Cupcake after school!" I call, but I don't think Alice hears.

After slipping my rucksack over my shoulders, I skip excitedly down the long corridor and then slide down the shiny brass handrail of the long marble staircase into the main entrance hall. I like the way the footmen try not to stare as I zoom past them.

When I reach the foot of the staircase I bend down and kiss Coco on her head. Then I exit through the side door I use to slip in and out of the palace without being gawped at by the tourists who gather by the main entrance.

I walk a little way through the gardens before turning towards a solid iron gate set within the old stone wall that runs round the castle. Here I wait for my police escort to give me the all-clear before I can pass through the gate (and they follow me out). The sentry guard on duty outside the castle wall (navy jacket with brass buttons, bright blue trousers and black bearskin hat, in case you're wondering about the uniform) is standing to attention in front of her red guardhouse and salutes me as I walk past.

I walk to school instead of being driven – and I bet you would too, if your only option was an enormous Rolls-Royce with accompanying driver in uniform, medals and cap. It's royally embarrassing!

Not that the palace was understanding when I first suggested it. Alice looked at me as if she thought using my legs to walk to school was an entirely new concept. Which I guess it was: "But no Crown Princess has ever walked to school." She pursed her lips. "Then again, no Crown Princess has ever gone to school outside the palace…"

In the end, police security stepped in and assured my mum that I'd be just as safe walking to school with a discreet escort as I'd be in the Rolls.

And good thing too, especially today. It gives me

a chance to think about everything that's happened since I woke up. After all, my day has only just started and yet I've already had two enormous surprises: Tiara Girl viewer numbers for my last video are now over two hundred! AND I'm going to wear a tiara on Friday night.

Plus I've decided I'm going to do a Tiara Girl video wearing a **REAL TIARA**!

So that's actually three enormous surprises!

I just have to make sure I don't get caught.

But surely I can come up with a good plan, right?

An Alice-proof, Grandmaman-proof plan, a no-one-in-the-palace-will-see-me kind of plan.

Right??

Right.

Chapter THREE

9.13 a.m., at school

I'm the first Waldenburg Crown Princess to go to school outside the palace. My mother was home-schooled in the former nursery located on the top floor of the palace – as was my grandmother, great-grandmother, great-great-grandmother and – well, you get the picture. People living outside the palace sometimes ask me how it feels to go to school – but how am I supposed to answer? I mean, stuff like homework is the same whether you're a princess or not.

I don't think I'm given any special treatment by Waldenburg Primary and Secondary School, even if I am going to rule Waldenburg one day. For instance, at school everyone calls me Lily Waldenburg. Nobody uses my full name (FYI: Her Royal Highness Lilian Athena Isabella Marie, the Crown Princess of Waldenburg).

Then again, every so often I get the feeling that my homework is scrutinized more than everyone else's. When I mentioned this to my mum, she said, "Well it should be. Being a queen is a job of constant – and public – evaluation, you know."

I'd never thought of it in those terms, but I guess Mum has a point. Although I can't say it's the kind of point that makes me count the days in excitement until I become queen myself.

FIVE THINGS YOU SHOULD KNOW ABOUT THE QUEENDOM OF WALDENBURG:

1. Waldenburg is the only queendom in existence in the world. According to our constitution, Waldenburg can only be ruled by a queen – and the eldest daughter is always first in line to the throne. Boys, in fact, are not in the line of

succession at all. Instead, Waldenburg princes – and younger daughters – have traditionally been given a good education and a property somewhere of their choosing. If there happens to be a generation in which no princesses are born – and this has happened only twice in our nine-hundred-year history – then the throne goes to the eldest niece of the reigning queen. There never has been, and there never will be, a *King* of Waldenburg. If, on the other hand, Waldenburg were a *kingdom*, then it would be ruled by a king.

2. Waldenburg has one of the most beautiful mountain ranges in Europe and is known as "die Perle der Berge" (that's "the pearl of the mountains" in German).

3. Speaking of which, the three official languages of Waldenburg are German, French and Waldenburgerish (a mix of Old German, French and Latin).

4. Men have been allowed to vote in Waldenburg since 1986. Prior to that only women had voting

rights. It was my grandfather who convinced Grandmaman to change the law. Grandmaman was reluctant, but she felt Waldenburg had to move with the times.

5. There is no fashion scene to speak of in Waldenburg.

Okay, maybe that last one isn't a fact you really need to know…but you can't seriously expect anyone with a love of style to live here and ignore this glaring national embarrassment, can you? I think this totally excuses my vlogging.

I'm supposed to be concentrating on history right now, but I'm so totally excited about the tiara video I'm going to do later this week that I can hardly sit through lessons! It's almost like I'm more excited about vlogging about wearing the tiara than I am about actually wearing it. New ideas keep popping into my head, like maybe I can make a new tiara for Coco to wear in the video with me?

Yesss!

Oh, and I've just had the best idea ever!

Last week I found a secret room in the palace.

At least I think it's a secret room…I've never seen anyone go in or out of it – and I've never heard my mum or Alice or Grandmaman mention it. And it's definitely abandoned because when I discovered it there were a ton of cobwebs all over it.

Anyway, I **LOVE** it! And I've been cleaning it so I can use it as my secret hideout – but maybe I should start *vlogging* in it… That would be far less risky than vlogging in my bedroom because it would mean Alice or Grandmaman or my mum couldn't just walk in, unannounced, while I'm filming.

Not unless they managed to find the secret entrance first (which is hidden behind an enormous antique Flemish tapestry hanging in the corridor outside my bedroom).

The thing is, if I film my upcoming special tiara vlog in my secret room then I'll need to jazz it up a bit.

But how can I make it look special? I mean **MORE** special. Because it already looks special – at least I think so. Or maybe it just feels so special because it's mine. Well, mine and Zoë and Coco's…I mean they found it…

I probably wouldn't have even noticed the secret entrance if Zoë hadn't escaped last week – right in the middle of filming my third Tiara Girl video.

When I film videos in my bedroom, I take down the picture that hangs between two of my windows and stand against the wall, holding my phone out in front of me. I know that doesn't sound like the most exciting backdrop…but I figure that with a nondescript wall behind me no one will be able to guess that I am in a palace.

Anyway, because of the boring background I include Zoë and Coco in my videos – they definitely make things more cute and fun – but it's not always easy to control them *and* film at the same time. Which is how Zoë escaped: I set her down on the floor for a moment, while I was adjusting something on my phone, and she made a run for the door – something she'd never done before.

It was almost as if she knew she had to show me the secret room – like even she thought I needed a new and more exciting location to film in. (Promise, cross my heart, she is the world's cleverest royal guinea pig ever.)

Coco followed her out and I followed Coco. Good thing too, because Zoë had vanished and without Coco I never would have found her. I watched as Coco disappeared behind the enormous tapestry – which is about five metres long and heavy (like a very large carpet, basically), and hangs from the ceiling to the floor. Then she started barking – which made me **REALLY** nervous because I didn't want anything alerting Mum or Grandmaman or Alice, in case they went into my bedroom and noticed that I'd moved a few things around for filming – not to mention that I had camera-ready make-up on. It would lead to **WAY** too many questions, which would mean I might just as well kiss my vlog goodbye.

I quickly slipped behind the tapestry, hoping Coco's barking meant she'd found Zoë, and turned on my phone torch. Fortunately she quietened down as soon as she saw me pushing my way along the wall towards her. It was very dusty behind the tapestry.

Just beyond Coco sat Zoë, still wearing the blush-pink tutu she'd had on for the video, calmly grooming herself, with her bottom squished against the wall behind her.

Only it wasn't a wall.

As I swept the beam of my torch around I noticed the outline of a door. It had no door frame and was painted to match the stones of the wall – just like the other secret doors we have in the castle (in the chapel, the ballroom and the library).

At this point I completely forgot about the video (Zoë's tutu was filthy with dust now anyhow) as seeing the secret door made me really curious to know what was behind it.

So I scooped Zoë up and pulled on the tiny door knob.

The door opened easily and led onto a narrow spiral staircase. As I stepped through the doorway, with Coco at my heels, I found a light switch on the wall to my right. I flipped it on and waited as a few of the light bulbs on the gilded torches lining the stairwell flickered very slowly to life. It was still quite dark (most of the lights weren't working) and cobwebs hung everywhere, but funnily enough, I didn't feel the least bit scared. I mean, yeah, sure, it was a bit weird finding out that all this time there was a hidden staircase just outside my bedroom…but it was exciting too!

I couldn't help but get a kick out of the fact that my bodyguard, police escort, the Court Master of Ceremonies, the Grand Chamberlain, Sandra, Alice, Grandmaman, my parents and everyone else in the palace would have **NO IDEA** where I was if I continued up the stairs.

So I shut the door behind me and climbed up the long and winding staircase. After a while I came to a short landing and a thick wooden door with a rounded top. The doorway isn't much taller than I am and a large gold key jutted out from the ornate, gilded lock on the door. I turned the key and stepped inside.

The room I walked into was amazing. It was round and bright with windows that had a bird's eye view over the mountains of Waldenburg. I realized I was in the palace's highest turret! I felt like a pirate on a ship's mast as all the forests of the queendom spread out in every direction, the steep green mountains like waves on the sea.

Far below me I could see the castle walls, laid out like a pretty necklace, encircling the old town centre and palace gardens. Beyond that the town of Waldenburg spilled down the steep slopes of the palace peak. Below me, falcons flew above the other turrets and far below that, in the Valley of the Queens, the Waldenburg River twinkled in the sunlight.

The walls of the room were a creamy white with light gold decoration on the panelling. And, like the ballroom, the ceiling was painted to look like the sky – only instead of cherubs there were all sorts of butterflies and birds. A crystal chandelier hung from its centre.

A free-standing, full-length mirror with an ornate gold frame, a dainty gold desk, and a huge, throne-like gilded chair with a pink velvet seat were the only pieces of furniture in the room.

It was perfect and I loved it. I didn't care that everything was covered in dust and cobwebs and the room was obviously abandoned – in fact, I loved it *because* it was abandoned.

That meant that finally – **FINALLY** – I had a place that was all mine.

A secret place that no one knew about.

The next day I cleaned it up as best I could. Trust me, though, if you're a princess, it's not easy to get hold of a mop and bucket. That's because princesses aren't supposed to do housework.

When I asked one of the cleaners about borrowing some cleaning equipment she immediately radioed the head of palace housekeeping. She in turn insisted on meeting me to ask, "Is there anything you are specifically displeased with, Your Royal Highness? If so you have only to say and I'll get the team onto it."

So I had to back down and say that I wasn't displeased about a thing! They did a splendid job and I'd only thought that perhaps it might amuse Zoë to climb around on a bucket and mop.

I know, it's not a great excuse, but it was the only

one I could think of in a hurry.

The housekeeper and cleaner looked at me with wide eyes but were too polite to say anything. I could see the housekeeper was nervous, though, so to stop her from calling Alice or anyone else in the palace office, I said my idea wasn't the best and suggested we just forget it – I'd find something else for Zoë to play with.

Later that night, when the cleaners had all left for the day and everyone thought I was asleep, I went to a housekeeping cupboard I knew about, found what I needed and got to work in my turret.

Luckily, nobody noticed a thing. So now all the cobwebs have gone, but if I'm going to use this room to film the tiara special on Friday I think I should decorate it too.

Because although my secret turret is now clean, it could look better.

I need to calm my mind so I can concentrate on my History lesson, but instead the decorating ideas start

flowing. I'd usually discuss things with Leonie, but she has a dental appointment this morning, and she's not answering the messages I've sent her. So I decide to write a list.

IDEAS FOR DECORATING MY SECRET TURRET:

1. Add fairy lights.
2. Paint round tower room pink.
3. What about a mood board? For my favourite inspiring images?
4. Maybe some stencilling? Like hearts or stars – or both.
5. Make sure nobody at the palace discovers I'm decorating an abandoned room.

Okay, so the last point on this list is not a decorating idea, but I can't let anyone get suspicious about my comings and goings. After all, it was difficult enough just getting a mop and bucket up there.

And how often does a princess walk around her

palace carrying paint cans and large brushes or ladders? **NEVER**, that's how often. Now you know what I'm up against.

★ Chapter FOUR

1.01 p.m., between Biology and Art

Leonie isn't feeling well after her dental appointment so she messages to say she's gone home for the rest of the day. Which means that not only do I still not have a decorating plan for my secret turret, but I can't even talk to Leonie about it because she has a huge wad of cotton in her mouth. She sent me a photo from the surgery. She looked like a hamster with stuffed cheek pouches.

But she loves my turret. She saw it over the weekend – I snuck her in and we spent an hour up there brainstorming for more super glittery DIY fashion projects. Yay!

When I texted to ask her about the fairy lights

she answered straight away:

Leonie: YES!

Me: And what about pink walls?

Leonie: YES!

Me: And a mood board?
And maybe some stencilling on
the walls too?

Leonie: Definitely!

Leonie brought up another good point:

Leonie: I think you need to start filming with
a proper camera and tripod. Especially now
you're getting more views. (SO EXCITING!)
Then you won't have to hold Zoë and you
can get all of Coco in the shots too. And
maybe we should write a script...?

I am suddenly very thankful that Leonie's an actor (she regularly gets the lead in our school plays) – even though that means she can sometimes be a major **DIVA**. Love her anyway! The point is, because of her passion for acting, Leonie knows all about camera angles, lighting and backdrops and scripts – basically all things I know nothing about – but really should if I want to keep vlogging...

Me: GREAT idea! Only I don't have a camera. And I don't want the palace getting curious about why I suddenly need one... I can ask for one for Christmas but that's three months away...

Leonie: No problem – we'll use mine. And I have a tripod – and I can bring some lights! Do you remember those collapsible ones Mum bought last year, so I could practise for that commercial I was cast in?

Me: You're the best!

Leonie: I know.

Me: Ha ha. But seriously, thank you.

We agree to call later and make a plan. As soon as the cotton wool is out of her mouth.

As I walk home from school, with a security escort behind me and one in front of me, I think back to the first time I vlogged.

It didn't cross my mind to hide my identity to start with. So it was a good thing I showed the video to Leonie before I uploaded it. Straight away she said, "First of all, you shouldn't call yourself Lily on your channel – not if you want your vlog to remain a secret. What if someone from school sees you? They'll know for sure it's you!"

Leonie was right – using my name on my vlogging channel would be too big of a giveaway. So we had a quick brainstorming session and I decided to call myself Tiara Girl on my vlog.

Then Leonie suggested that I also make myself look different on my vlog to how I look in real life.

"You have to make sure that no Waldenburger will recognize you if they find your channel," she said.

"But all the best vloggers say you should be yourself when you vlog!" I protested.

"Most vloggers aren't future queens with a country to think about," Leonie answered. Her big blue eyes looked very intense. Sometimes Leonie can sound a lot like Alice. "Imagine what Alice will do to you if she finds out you're secretly vlogging about fashion!"

"I'd rather not think about it."

"Then you'd better find a way to hide your identity."

"But how am I supposed to be myself when I'm wearing a disguise?" I asked.

Leonie tied her curly dark hair up in a bun and then walked to my wardrobe and started digging around. "It's not a disguise! Just dress how you really want to – not how Princess Lily is supposed to. You're always saying that your parents and the palace and Alice are always telling you how to dress – well, your channel is YOUR chance to decide what you want to wear! With Tiara Girl you can be a royal rebel and no one will know!"

"Actually, Leonie, that's a brilliant idea!" I said as I tried on the heart-shaped glasses she'd just pulled out of my wardrobe.

"I know," Leonie answered.

I lobbed a cushion at her head.

THIS IS WHAT I WEAR WHEN I'M TIARA GIRL:

1. Pink heart-shaped sunglasses.
2. Pink wig. (From last year's Halloween costume when Leonie and I dressed as pink vampires.)
3. My own clothes. These are tops and skirts and jeans and things that I've customized with ribbon and sparkles and fabric patches. I think they're really cute, although they'd probably give my grandmother and Alice a heart attack

if they saw me wearing them. My customized clothes have never made it beyond the palace gates so they're perfect for me to vlog in – no one can possibly recognize them!

Of course, I suppose someone watching my videos might recognize Coco...then again, half the time she's wearing some kind of outfit I've made her in the videos too, so it wouldn't be that easy – even for Waldenburgers who sometimes see me walking her through town.

I don't worry much about Zoë because most Waldenburgers don't even know I have a guinea pig.

When I get home Coco is waiting for me, her nails clicking on the marble floor as she jumps around, tail wagging.

Alice is also waiting for me.

"Princess Lily, don't forget that you and I will meet later for your first Princess Class – straight after you've been riding *and* finished your homework." She lifts a file of papers. "We need to go over the biographies of the guests coming for dinner on Friday."

The way Alice says "the guests coming for dinner on Friday" almost tricks me into thinking I'll be attending a casual picnic in our private garden. Which I won't be.

I'll be attending a **MEGA-FORMAL DINNER** in one of the grandest rooms in the palace!

I thank Alice and tell her I'll see her later. Then I quickly dash up the stairs to my bedroom to change, Coco at my heels.

As I head to my bedroom all sorts of thoughts about Friday night whizz through my mind. I mean, the possibilities for things to go royally wrong are endless...

Like, what if my tiara slips off my head as I walk into the dining hall, just as the band starts to play and everyone stands up to watch me walk in? Or what if I try to spear a cherry tomato with my fork and it accidentally goes flying across the table at the very same moment my mother stands up to make her speech? Worse yet, what if I trip over and fall flat on my you-know-what just as I walk past the Waldenburg television cameras that will be filming the event live?

Now you know the kind of pressure I'm under; any little mistake and Waldenburgers might start to think that their future queen is too accident-prone to lead the country.

I'm telling you, the whole princess thing is not so easy-peasy.

I take a deep breath as I turn into my bedroom and tell myself that I'll be fine on Friday night, that it will be fun speaking English and French and German and Spanish and even my broken Italian.

Really, it will.

But what will absolutely definitely be extra fun, I remind myself as I walk into my bedroom and quickly take Zoë out of her cage for a snuggle, before changing into my riding gear, is that I'll get to wear a real tiara on Friday night – and *then* I'll secretly vlog about it!

A ROYAL FACT THAT MOST PEOPLE ARE (PROBABLY) UNAWARE OF:

No queen or king, or heir to the throne, is ever allowed to go horse riding on their own. **EVER**.

And because I'm Crown Princess, that includes me.

I've never been allowed to ride on my own. As my mother, Grandmaman and Alice put it: "You are the heir to the throne, Lily. It is too risky. Something might happen to you and then what? Your palace security must ride with you."

Then, if I so much as look as if I'm going to say something – which I am – they finish with: "And there will be no discussion about it."

This is something my mum and dad always say. I know Leonie's parents like to say it too, so maybe it's not just a royal thing, but more of a universal parent thing.

Last year I saw a photo in a gossip magazine of a European Crown Prince and his wife riding through the park of their summer palace, with not a police officer in sight. I pointed this out to Alice.

The next day Alice showed me a different photo – one that the palace of the young couple in question had sent her. This photo showed that there were three police officers pedalling furiously behind the Crown Prince couple on bicycles.

I'm used to it now, though. Everyone on my security team is really kind and they try to stay as far behind me as possible. Sometimes, like on windy forest bridle paths, I almost have the feeling that I'm alone. Besides, Cupcake is the sweetest pony in the world and riding her is magical.

FYI: Cupcake's a palomino Waldenburger Mountain Pony with a blaze and four white stockings on her legs. She has a soft brown nose and large, very dark brown eyes. Her mane and tail are thick and luxurious. And riding her definitely makes me feel about as free as I'll ever feel – except when I'm vlogging.

I ride for an hour through the woods surrounding the castle and Coco keeps up the whole way. But then I hear the clock bell in the stable chime and that means it's time to return to the palace and meet Alice for my Princess Class.

Alice is on the phone, waiting for me in Grandmaman's small sitting room – the one in her private wing of the palace. The room is a pretty powder-blue colour, with high ceilings, delicate gilded furniture and windows that look over the rose garden below. Today is a warm September afternoon and the windows are open, allowing the scent of the roses to waft into the room. Roses always remind me of my grandmother.

I can hear her talking on the phone from her adjacent bedroom as I flop, face down, onto a silk-covered sofa, while Alice paces the other end of the room, still on her phone. Coco jumps on the sofa with me and we're both having fun, seeing how many of Grandmaman's plump, embroidered cushions I can squish under my jumper, when I suddenly hear Alice cough.

She's standing over me with the same sheaf of papers she waved at me earlier.

"Princess Lilian," she says, "it's time to begin. And may I suggest you place the cushions back where you found them?"

FYI: when Alice suggests something, it's basically an order.

"We can sit at the table by the window," she adds as she waves her papers in the direction of a small card table where my grandmother often plays solitaire and bridge.

I can feel Alice watching me as I walk to the table, and I know what she's going to say before she says it.

"Back straight," we both speak at the same time.

Alice purses her lips. "It's for your own good, Lily. Your coming of age will be upon us soon and from that point forward your life will become one of increased scrutiny. Every one of your actions will reflect upon your family and the nine hundred years of Waldenburg history you represent. So it's not a moment too soon to begin with your Princess Classes."

FOUR THINGS I KNOW WILL HAPPEN WHEN I TURN FOURTEEN:

1. My entire life will be scheduled and I will have to be on time, always, everywhere, **FOR THE**

REST OF MY LIFE. Even brushing my teeth will become a scheduled event.

2. According to Grandmaman, I will become a living piece of Waldenburg history. I have no idea what this means, but it **DEFINITELY** doesn't sound like fun.

3. I will have to give lots of speeches in front of hundreds of people. If this doesn't freak you out, then you aren't human.

4. I might as well kiss glitter goodbye. No future monarch and head of state does glitter in any way, shape or form. Even glittery eyeshadow is pushing it. I know because I heard my mother say so once.

By the time I sit down at the card table I've come to the following conclusion: **MY LIFE WILL BE OVER WHEN I TURN FOURTEEN.**

My life is over **NOW**.

Alice has spent two hours talking to me about what

subjects a princess can and cannot talk about at dinner and in what order the guests will walk into the Tapestry Hall when we have dinner on Friday night.

She's also making me take notes.

THREE SUBJECTS ALICE SAYS A PRINCESS CAN TALK ABOUT:

1. The weather. I said to Alice that this was a particularly boring subject and couldn't we exchange it for something like my favourite celebrity's acting career? Alice said that future heads of state don't discuss celebrities and that I should ask my dinner partner how they find the weather. I told Alice that maybe lightning will strike and I'll find a more interesting subject. Ha ha! She didn't get my joke.

2. Any hobby my dinner partner may have, such as gardening. I know what their hobbies are because Alice has given me a copy of the guests' biographies. There are surprisingly few who ride or have dogs or even guinea pigs (let

alone a style vlog). Alice says this doesn't matter because I'm supposed to talk to them about *their* hobbies, not mine. This dinner is sounding less fun with every passing moment.

3. Culture. Such as any art exhibition or concert I have recently been to. Alice also says that it's nice to flatter a guest by mentioning something about the culture of their country. I tell Alice thank you very much but I'll stick to the first two subjects because I don't know enough about the cultures of the world. But as soon as I say this, I wish I hadn't because Alice says not to worry, that she has a lovely surprise for me later. This *does* worry me because, apart from the miniature hamster that she brought me back from a state visit to Mongolia (for my fifth birthday), Alice's idea of a "lovely surprise" is usually very different from *my* idea of a lovely surprise.

I try to distract myself from the worrying thought of Alice's surprise by planning the miniature tiara I will make Coco for my video on Friday. I think I'll string clear crystal beads because they look like white diamonds. And I have some pink crystal beads I can add too, so that it will match the Queen Josephine Pink Diamond Tiara I'll be wearing!

YAY!

8 p.m., still in Grandmaman's sitting room

Yes, my life is definitely over.

I'm just about to leave Grandmaman's sitting room when Alice informs me that my daily Princess Class will be supplemented with additional weekly classes in Waldenburg History and Political Science.

Starting tomorrow.

With **PROFESSOR WALTRAUD HUSTEMEIER**.

(And Alice, of course.)

"But I'm learning those subjects in school!" I say.

Alice fixes her steely blue eyes on me. "That's as may be, Lily, but as the future queen of this country you need to know your queendom's history better than anyone else – and that means in-depth study of the sort you don't get in school. And, as a future queen and head of state, you will be the person who signs laws into existence; not to mention the fact that after your official coming of age you will also be able to act as regent when your mother is away. Therefore, I can hardly overemphasize how important it is that you know the ins and outs of Waldenburg politics." Alice pauses, then adds, "You'll have fun. The country you will one day inherit is a very interesting one."

I ask Alice if she really thinks that anyone with a name like Waltraud Hustemeier could make anything fun or interesting. Alice says that I must put my duty to Waldenburg before fun, and that after a long interview process it was clear to the palace and my mother that Waltraud Hustemeier was the person to help me. She also reminds me that I should never judge anyone upon their name alone.

She has a point. I don't like it when people assume that, because I'm a princess, I must swan around all day in a long dress and have Rapunzel-like golden locks and blue eyes – when in fact I mostly wear jeans (when I'm not in school) and have shoulder-length brown hair, dark brown eyes and olive skin.

Then Alice says that of course it will be fun anyway because she'll also be there.

Because of the shock to my system that this comment causes I am unable to reply.

Once I'm back in my bedroom I message Leonie about this new development but she thinks it's hilarious. And then she asks if Professor Hustemeier can help us with our homework. Leonie's message annoys me so I don't message her back. Until I remember that she's supposed to help me decorate my secret turret tomorrow.

I message her back.

> Me: Ha ha! Very Funny. Now let's talk about serious things, like my secret turret DIY project.

Leonie: YES! And I won't forget my camera and tripod, or the lights. Your Tiara video special is going to look so awesome!

Me: It's so exciting. Btw, I found some spare fairy lights in my wardrobe, left over from when I hung them in my bedroom...but where do you think I can get the pink paint?

Leonie: Good question... I don't know. No, wait! Dickel's Hardware Shop. I'm sure I've seen paint in their windows.

Leonie and I decide that we'll go straight to Dickel's after school, and after we have the paint we'll go to the palace and my secret turret.

And hopefully nobody will suspect anything unusual.

Chapter Five

7.22 a.m., Tuesday, in my bedroom

Hi Tiara Girl! And welcome to your channel!

Your most recent video:

<u>Tiara Girl's Top Three Back-to-School</u>
<u>Hairstyles</u> has had:

987 views

WHAT!?

I quickly check my first three vlogs and they've all gone up – **WAY** up – in views, too. I'm so excited when I see this that I take Zoë out of her cage and hold her to me as I twirl around my room. Coco watches me from the bed and barks encouragement.

I'm about to message Leonie when Sandra knocks at my door to say that my grandmother will be at breakfast at eight o'clock and would like to see me.

Royal duty calls.

"Lily, sit down, please," Grandmaman says when I walk into the small dining room.

Today she is wearing a yellow dress, with a large flower-shaped brooch of different-coloured gemstones on her left shoulder and her ever-present black patent-leather handbag and white gloves beside her.

My mum is also at breakfast. I haven't seen her since she left to go to Brazil for her state visit, so I fling myself at her as soon as I see her and she holds me tightly; after saying how much she's missed me she asks me how I've been. She is looking very regal in an orange knee-length dress under a beige lace coat, with a matching hat. High heels, gloves, an orange clutch bag and a large brooch and matching earrings finish off her queenly look. She's always perfectly accessorized and coordinated and very polished. And she smells like a fresh meadow. Mum's outfits are also always totally "appropriate" (as Alice repeatedly reminds me), whether she's opening Parliament in her royal regalia (crown, sceptre and orb) or meeting the Waldenburg Girl Guides in the forest for a fire-making demonstration.

I can see why my dad totally fell in love with her when they met at the Winter Olympics (Dad represented Mexico in the Skiing) when they were held in Waldenburg.

"We've asked to see you this morning, Lily," Mum says, "to tell you that to mark your coming of age the post office has been in touch with the palace. Can you guess why?"

I immediately get excited because I know that when my mother had her official coming of age, the sheik of a faraway desert kingdom sent her an all white Arabian mare as a birthday present. But when I suggest that it might have something to do with shipping me a horse from a desert kingdom, my grandmother and mum only look startled.

My second guess is that maybe I'm being sent a cocker spaniel from the Royal Kennels at Sandringham in England. I cover Coco's ears when I say this because I don't want her getting jealous.

Grandmaman sounds exasperated when she tells me it has absolutely nothing to do with sending me a horse or a dog or a birthday present and that honestly by now I should know that it has to do with my stamp.

Yes, my **STAMP**.

As in the one with my image on it, which will be produced by the Royal Waldenburg Post to mark my coming of age.

HOW EMBARRASSING!!!

Although a more fun thought quickly comes to mind; every Waldenburg stamp with Grandmaman, Mum or any other Waldenburg queen always shows them in full formal dress. So surely this means that I get to wear a ballgown and tiara on my stamp, too!

70

Excitedly, I pull a notebook out of my backpack and start to sketch a design. When Grandmaman asks me what I'm doing, I tell her that if I'm going to have my portrait taken for a stamp, then perhaps I can design my own ballgown to wear. And maybe even make it myself!

Mum smiles and shakes her head and says she doubts there will be time for me to design and make a dress, because my portrait will be taken within the next two weeks. Then, after reminding me to have a good day at school and to concentrate in my Princess Class, she tells me that Dad wants to walk with me to school this morning. Then she says she'll see me later, kisses me goodbye and turns to leave just as my breakfast arrives.

I go back to my sketchbook as I spoon the last few blueberries and porridge out of my bowl. Grandmaman watches me for a moment but doesn't say anything. Then she looks at her watch and says, "We'll talk about your clothes for the portrait another day, Lily.

We haven't chosen the photographer yet, so right now, I'd suggest you finish your orange juice and get going. Nobody likes a princess who is late."

As I stand up to leave, Grandmaman says, "May I have a look at your drawing, Lily?"

I hand it to her.

"It's quite a good sketch," she says. Then, after a minute, she hands my notebook back to me and says mysteriously, "I think I've just had a brilliant idea."

"Yes, Grandmaman?"

"Nothing, Lily, nothing. Go on now and have a good day at school. I have a concert I must attend tonight – in honour of the Waldenburg Firefighters' Association – so I'll see you briefly at your Princess Class before I leave."

What can Grandmaman mean by "I've just had a brilliant idea", I wonder as I leave the dining room. The way she was looking at me when she said it makes me feel it's got something to do with me.

I'm curious, but it's time to go…

Dad walks beside me as we cross the palace garden and make our way out through the small iron gate in the palace wall. We walk discreetly past the early morning tourists taking pictures of the palace. Once we're off the palace compound we talk about my parents' state visit to Brazil and Dad tells me about all the funny things that happened on the trip – like how the lady sitting on his right at the state gala dinner fell asleep during one particularly long and boring speech.

But just before we reach the school gates Dad stops and hugs me goodbye – he has a meeting with one of the charities he works with, so he has to go back to the palace. He blows me a kiss, then turns.

Leonie is waiting for me on the front steps of our school when I arrive, and she's brought her camera, tripod and the collapsible lights. She's also walked past Dickel's Hardware Shop and seen all kinds of paint samples in their window display. "Including some nice pink ones," she says.

"I'm so excited, it's going to be almost impossible to sit through school today!" I tell her.

"I know," Leonie agrees. "I feel exactly the same."

This is why we're besties!

As we walk to form room together I have another great idea! I'm going to do a DIY vlog! And it will be about the makeover I'm going to give my secret turret room. Leonie can film me while I'm working this afternoon and I'll be able to show viewers how to add a touch of glitter and fun to any room. And I know just the outfit I'll wear: my super-cute customized dungarees! They have patches all over them and are honestly the **BEST THING** you have ever seen.

If you don't count Cupcake in her glitter halter.

And Zoë in her mini tiara.

And Coco always.

Later in Maths, while Madame Roux drones on about geometry, I decide to design and cut some stencils to use when I decorate my secret turret. Fortunately I have a high pile of books at the front of my desk so Madame Roux doesn't notice a thing as I'm cutting a heart out of the middle of a sheet of thick white paper that I brought with me from home. I cut a second, larger heart and then two different-sized stars as well. They look great! I can't wait to start stencilling!

Chapter SIX

3.35 p.m., in town

School is finally out and Leonie and I (and my security team) are on our way to Dickel's Hardware Shop. My police security follow me everywhere and keep note of wherever I go…but they don't always have to know the real reason I'm going where I go. Which is why I've told them that it's *Leonie* who has to go to the hardware shop.

Which actually, she does – to help me!

Shhh!

I know I'm Crown Princess of Waldenburg and everything, but, honestly, I think Waldenburg town is really pretty.

THREE REASONS WHY WALDENBURG TOWN LOOKS LIKE A FAIRY TALE:

1. Waldenburg's buildings are all made of stone or half timbering and each one is different from the one next to it. Some are so old that they lean out at crazy angles and you have to wonder how they stay standing.

2. Many buildings are painted in pretty pastel colours. And most are quite small with tiny windows and doors. That's because people were smaller in the olden days.

3. There is a very high stone wall that goes all the way around Waldenburg – both the palace and the town. The walls have thirty watchtowers between them: twelve on the palace walls and eighteen on the town walls. This is from back when the first queens of Waldenburg were constantly being attacked. I'm happy those days are over!

I bet you're wondering if everyone

in downtown Waldenburg recognizes me as I walk around. This is a question I'm regularly asked, and the answer is, yes, pretty much.

Waldenburgers recognize me because they've seen pictures of me since I was born: me at my christening, my official first birthday photos, my official second birthday photos (all of my official birthday photos, basically), my first day at school, the first day of my second year at school…you get the picture.

So they definitely know who I am.

But I also think that most people try to leave me alone when they see me doing normal stuff like buying an ice cream or walking to school. They might say something nice as they pass me, or call out "Princess Lilian", but it's pretty low-key. So I don't get too much attention as Leonie and I head to the hardware shop.

I've found the **PERFECT** shade of pink for my secret turret room. Leonie and are super excited until we speak to Frau Dickel, the shopkeeper, and explain how big the room we need to paint is – basically about the size of the hardware shop, but double the height.

We don't say it's in the palace, but I can see Frau Dickel raise an eyebrow as Leonie describes the dimensions of "her bedroom".

She says that in order to paint a room of that size, we're going to need many more cans of paint than we can carry. This is not a good idea because if I need a car to transport it all to the palace, then I will definitely be asked all kinds of questions. Besides, I suddenly realize we'd need ladders to paint the whole room and there's no way Leonie and I could sneak huge ladders into my turret.

I don't know what to do…

But then I have a brainwave. We'll take two small "test-size" cans of paint, because that's all we can fit into our backpacks, and I'll use the heart and star stencils I made in Maths to create a feature wall instead of painting the entire room. I choose two smallish paintbrushes – one for each of us – and then hand Leonie my pocket money. She pays at the till so that Frau Dickel believes it's for her bedroom.

The Dickels are very nice and know who I am, and Herr Dickel even tells me that my mother looked beautiful in the purple dress she wore the other day when she toured the hospital where Frau Dickel's sister works as a doctor. Thankfully, he stops just as my ears start burning from embarrassment; there are a few people in the queue behind us listening to Herr Dickel and staring at me at the same time.

Back at the palace, we decide to take the lift upstairs because we're carrying so much. I smile to the footmen who open the door for me but then Leonie and I sneak across the Marble Hall and use the lift near the Guards Gallery, which is the one nearest to my bedroom. As the lift takes off Leonie asks me if I know who the secret turret room used to belong to.

"No I don't," I say. "And the problem is that I can't ask anyone like my grandmother, or Alice, or the head of the palace buildings, because then they'll be curious to find out how I know about it and that will be the end of my secret."

Leonie agrees I mustn't ever mention the secret turret room to anyone.

Except her, of course.

We decide to do our homework as quickly as we can and then decorate, so as soon as we're in my bedroom we both lie on the floor and start. Not surprisingly, Alice comes to check on us. Fortunately, Leonie and I are hard at work on our science homework and not dancing on my bed with the music turned up.

Alice looks pleased.

Until she spots something.

"What is wrong with her? She has something on her head. What is it?" she says as she points to Zoë, who is running loose around my bedroom in her ruby tiara. Okay, so they are fake rubies, but they are *real* crystals and they're red, so that's why I call it her Ruby Tiara.

Alice looks as if she's never seen a guinea pig wearing a tiara. Which I guess she hasn't. I try to explain that because I finally get to wear a tiara it seems only fair that Zoë gets to wear one too. But Alice is not amused. In fact she looks really cross and says that it's indecent to mix up nine hundred years of royal heritage with a guinea pig. But I say that Zoë is a royal guinea pig because she lives in a palace. So she's part of the heritage.

Now Alice looks like a thunderstorm.

In case you haven't noticed, Alice has **NO** sense of humour.

Then, as she turns to leave, she says, "Speaking of heritage, Professor Hustemeier and I will enjoy enlightening you at your Princess Class this evening." So I guess the last laugh is on me because I had **TOTALLY** forgotten about my class tonight and Professor Hustemeier.

That is so **NOT** funny.

Leonie and I finish our homework and it's finally time to start my secret turret **DIY**.

I'm still in my school clothes, but my dungarees and the rest of my Tiara Girl outfit are in my rucksack

– along with a can of paint, the paintbrushes, stencils and a couple of the fairy-light boxes. Plus, for my mood board, I've got a folder of super-cute pictures I've taken with the pastel green Polaroid camera my parents gave me for Christmas, as well as some of my all-time favourite and most inspiring fashion images.

Zoë is in the pocket of my rucksack, with just her head poking out. She's so cute!

Leonie has a can of paint, some small portable speakers, and the camera in her rucksack. And the third fairy-light box. 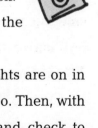 Plus she's carrying her tripod and the portable lights.

Before we go I make sure all the lights are on in my bedroom and I turn some music on too. Then, with Coco at my heels, we open the door and check to make sure the coast is clear, before we tiptoe to the large tapestry and slip underneath it.

We stay as flat as possible against the wall and move quickly and quietly until we arrive at the secret door in the wall.

PHEW!

Every time I go to my secret turret I get excited because it means freedom. And I know even Coco feels the same because she dashes ahead as we come round the last turn of the spiral staircase and stands barking at the top, her tail wagging.

I turn the golden key in the lock of the small wooden door, step into the room and stand for a moment. The sun is still high outside and the late afternoon light is flooding in, making the room dance with sunbeams. I walk to one of the windows looking out over the queendom.

"I love it up here!" Leonie exclaims. "It's like being alone at the very top of the world."

"You're right, Leonie, that's **EXACTLY** how it feels," I say as I start changing into my dungarees, sunglasses, pink wig and tiara. Once I'm ready, I look into the large gold-framed mirror leaning against the wall and smile. I am Tiara Girl. I am a royal rebel!

Leonie is talking about camera angles and morning light versus afternoon light and how to position my face when filming. I just nod because she is very clever about these kinds of things. "That's because I'm an actor," she says.

Leonie films me while I open a can of the paint and start stirring it.

"Now look at me and don't forget to talk us through what you're doing!" Leonie orders.

The stencils are really easy to use and I can't wait for my viewers to see the results, because I think that stencilling is a great way to personalize a room. I stencil a ton of pink hearts and stars across one of the spaces between two windows. Then I use double-sided tape to stick my Polaroid pictures directly onto a different wall. This is a super-easy way to create a mood board, because you don't actually need a board. I tape the pictures into the shape of a huge heart and it looks so cool that I decide to frame my mood board heart with fairy lights.

Leonie films some close-ups of Zoë while we unpack the fairy lights. She's still wearing her Ruby Tiara and she looks totally adorable as she weaves her way in and out of the lit-up fairy-light strands that are lying on the floor.

Leonie shows me the footage and it's clear
Zoë's a natural!

I hang fairy lights around my mood-board heart
with the white wall pins I've brought. Then I hang
some lights on the wall I've stencilled. "Don't hang
the fairy lights too straight," I say to the camera. "Add
some loops for fun."

"Hmmm…" I say as I stand back from the wall.
Leonie's still filming. "Something's missing… I
know!"

I take a paintbrush and, in large bold strokes,
paint the words **"Tiara Girl"** in loopy cursive script
straight onto the wall where the fairy lights hang.

YAY!

My secret turret room…

Looks…

Amazing!!!

Leonie and I turn some music on and dance around
to celebrate. And I don't have to worry about Alice
or Grandmaman surprising us because **THEY DON'T
KNOW WHERE I AM!
OR WHAT I'M DOING!**

"VLOGGING IS MY DESTINY!" I say at the top of my voice as I twist and turn.

I keep singing this until I happen to look at my phone and see what time it is and realize that my other destiny is waiting for me!

I'm late for Princess Class.

Alice is going to **KILL ME**!

Chapter SEVEN

6 p.m., Princess Class in Grandmaman's sitting room

I make it to my Princess Class just on time, only because I've changed out of my Tiara Girl disguise so quickly and run as fast as I could all the way here. By the time I swing open the door into Grandmaman's powder-blue sitting room, I'm red in the face and, I'll admit, my hair is a bit all over the place.

Apparently, I also have a large smudge of pink paint on my face, which Grandmaman notices immediately and tries to rub off.

How come I haven't noticed it?

And why didn't Leonie tell me about it?

Then I remember: Leonie had said something about the smudge, but that we should leave it because it looked "authentic" and "real" on film.

So we'd left it.

And then I'd forgotten all about it.

"Umm...that? Oh, that's just from my Art lesson this afternoon," I answer, and I feel bad because, honestly, in the whole history of fairy tales has there ever been even **ONE** good princess who lies?

About anything?

No.

But Grandmaman seems to believe me because she introduces me to Professor Waltraud Hustemeier and then leaves me with her and Alice.

I take a deep breath and sit down to learn all about Waldenburg history.

Everything, that is, that I haven't learned in the last **SIX YEARS** since I've been going to school. Seriously, how much more can there be to know?

It's actually more interesting than I thought. Not that I will ever admit that to Alice or Professor Hustemeier – even though I'm kind of starting to admire the professor's retro outfit of mismatched corduroy separates. (She's basically doing vintage without knowing it, which is kind of cool.)

But still...who knew that Waldenburg is a Mecca for girl power? Or that once upon a time many more countries and societies besides Waldenburg were ruled by women?

So what happened?

After all, Waldenburg has managed to survive nine hundred years of war, plagues, and the shenanigans of the ghost of Count Eberhart – not to mention uninspiring fashion – all thanks to women leaders.

Okay, so the bit about surviving uninspiring fashion has not been mentioned by Alice, but still... surely being a fashion backwater is a challenge for any country?

NOTES ON WALDENBURG AND GIRL POWER:

* Waldenburg is a matriarchal society and a *queendom*, which basically means that it is run

by women. If Waldenburg was ruled by men, then it would be a patriarchal society and a *kingdom*.

* Because of our status as the only queendom in existence, Waldenburg is a place of "special interest" to anyone studying feminism, which is basically girl power for adults.

* At Waldenburg University you can study all kinds of feminist subjects like: "How Women Have Shaped The World"; "Nine Hundred Years of Awesome Female Leadership"; "Channel Your Inner Queen" and many more.

* Waldenburg is a "matrilineal" society. This means that when a man marries he takes the surname of his wife. Apparently this is not the norm everywhere else in the world, don't ask me why.

* In Waldenburg, kids also take their mother's surname. For instance, if my BFF, Leonie Leonberger, had been born in France or America, both of which are "patrilineal" societies, she would most likely be called Leonie

Tewolde, because in those countries children usually take the father's surname. And while I know Ethiopia is a wonderful country, and Mr Leonburger (Tewolde) is a super-smart diplomat and everything...honestly, Leonie Tewolde does not have the same ring to it as Leonie Leonberger. Especially if you want to be an actor. Also, in Waldenburg all titles pass through the mother. So Alice, who is Alice Victoria, Countess of Vendelstein, got her title from her mum. And when Alice dies, her title will pass to her heiress (Alice has no children of her own, so it will go to her eldest niece). In Waldenburg, titles do not pass to men.

My world view has been totally flipped upside down because of all of this new knowledge. I mean, I knew that our neighbouring countries were different from us...but I hadn't realized that men had *quite* so much **POWER** in so much of the world...

Why? And how did it happen?

I think women need to band together and follow

Waldenburg's example because, obviously, they make better leaders and the world would be a much better place today if women were just left to get on with leading while the men did other things, like...like... Actually, I can't think of anything that men do better than women, although Mr Leonberger (Tewolde) always beats us at minigolf.

"Maybe in the future there will be more women leaders like ours," I say.

"There should be," Alice says. "Anyway, you will definitely become one, which is why you must learn as much as you can now. So that when the time comes, you will be an inspiring queen; one who reminds everyone that inside every girl is a born leader." Alice stops to look at her watch. "But now I think it's time for you to get ready for dinner, Lily. I know you're eating alone, but a princess never keeps anyone waiting – and that includes the palace staff."

I've finished my dinner and am back in my room, editing the video footage Leonie took of me earlier.

My **DIY** video is going to look amazing! I add some music at the opening bit, where I have spliced in the scene of Zoë running around the fairy lights, with her tiara on her head. Then I speed up some of the bits of me painting, and hanging the fairy lights, and zoom in and out for added effect. I also add in star and heart stickers and more graphics and music and it all looks **AMAZING**.

I cut the bits I don't think are interesting enough, so in the end the video is about four minutes long. The last shot you see before it fades out is a close-up of me in front of the Tiara Girl letters I painted on the wall, with the fairy lights hanging behind me. Zoë is sitting on my shoulder, and although my wig is a mess, my dungarees look super fabulous!

Finally, I upload the video to my channel.

And force myself to go to bed and **NOT** watch how many views my video gets within the first half-hour. Just the first fifteen minutes.

After that I turn my laptop off because I know that my mum or dad will come in to check on me as soon as they're back home from their official engagement and that might be any moment now. But a short while later Leonie messages me to let me know that she's seen the video and loves it, and that so far it has had 414 views and lots of comments.

414 views!

In only thirty minutes.

Leonie: They love the walls. And Zoë. And Zoë's tiara. Oh, and your dungarees. Some viewers are asking where they can buy them. And they're saying how FABULOUS THE VIDEO LOOKS!

Me: It looks fab because of all your help!

Leonie: I KNOW!

Leonie always thinks that whatever she does is fabulous. This is one of the things I love about her because it makes her lots of fun to be around. I wish her self-confidence would rub off on me!

I send her a few and then we make plans to meet up at school tomorrow morning, first thing.

Then I kiss Coco and Zoë goodnight.

Chapter EIGHT

7.03 a.m., Wednesday, at the palace

Hi Tiara Girl! And welcome to your channel!

Your most recent video:

<u>Tiara Girl's Tips For Your Own DIY Room</u>

has had:

3,036 views

I can't help but double-check my laptop to make sure the screen is clean.

It is.

3,036 views!

It's royally real!

But when I arrive at school Leonie is waiting for me on the front steps and she looks worried.

"Umm...I think I should warn you about something..." But just as she's about to tell me what she means, the large glass doors behind her suddenly swing open and a loud group of boys step out. They're waving signs and chanting, "We want rights!"

Then their leader spots me. Tall and lanky, with light brown hair and intense blue eyes, he moves towards me, and when he reaches me, he thrusts a paper into my hand and says, "Lilian Waldenburg, when you become queen you need to commit to helping men get equal rights!"

But before I can say or do anything, Leonie takes me by the arm and pulls me indoors.

"It's Political Awareness Week for some of the school clubs," Leonie says, as we head to our first class.

I'd completely forgotten. After sitting down I take out my folder, pencil and pen, and notebook, quietly un-crumple the paper and read it:

Waldenburg School's Boys' Movement
It's time to fight!

We won't stop until we've achieved equal rights for the male citizens of Waldenburg! Fellow Waldenburg students, these are questions you should ask yourselves:

1. Why do we always have a queen? What's wrong with having a king?
2. Why do Waldenburger families always take the mother's surname? It's time to change this tradition!
3. Us guys don't get to have a say over anything! Why do women and girls always call the shots in Waldenburg?
4. Why are 75% of our Parliament Members women? What about us? Waldenburg needs political equality!

Fellow Waldenburg students, it's your responsibility to join us in our fight for gender equality!

#boysarepeopletoo

I'm definitely being directly targeted with this memo. I mean, look at point number one.

As if I don't have enough to think about what with my vlog and Princess Classes and Friday night's formal dinner and my face going on stamps and everything!

I take a deep breath and read through the memo again. It does have some valid points – although it's going to take a lot more than me becoming queen to change things. Grandmaman sometimes tells me that every queen has her issues (meaning national ones, during her reign). As I fold the memo away, I can't help but feel that the main issue of my future reign might very well be equal rights – for all Waldenburgers, especially boys and men...

I pass Leonie a note asking if she knew there was a boys' movement at school but she just shakes her head and mouths "no". Then she passes me a note saying she's heard that it's just been formed and that a new student named Max started it. Apparently, he was living in America before returning to Waldenburg with his family (his mother is a Waldenburger).

Also, like Leonie, he's a member of our school's student drama club and, Leonie says, Max has already been vocal about all the good roles going to girls.

After our lesson Leonie tells me she has a Drama Club meeting during lunch – and she has to take her little brother to the doctor's straight after school, so I won't see her until tomorrow.

It's lunchtime, and just when I thought my life couldn't possibly squeeze in any more developments, a new one has come via the message box of my Tiara Girl account.

This is a super-fantastic extra-special development and **I AM THRILLED TO BITS!**

On my way to the school cafeteria I stop to check on Tiara Girl (5,554 views on my new **DIY** vlog, by the way! **FIVE THOUSAND!** Plus, all of my videos put together now total over 30,000 views!) and see a message from **Teen Me** – **YES, THAT Teen Me**, the most super-cool and amazing teen **MAGAZINE** anywhere on the planet!

They want to interview me – as Tiara Girl – for a story on newbie vloggers.

Here's the best part: they have no idea that Tiara Girl is *me* – Her Royal Highness Lilian Athena Isabella Marie, The Crown Princess of Waldenburg.

Which is what is **SO** cool!

Like, no one has ever, ever, asked me to talk about something besides being a Crown Princess. So although I've done several interviews, usually once a year, on my birthday…they've always been "princess" interviews, where the questions are all about what it's like to grow up as a Crown Princess. As if that alone is what's most interesting about me…and while I know that for some people it is, I also know that there's more to me than just my name.

And **Teen Me** agrees!

I'm so excited that without waiting another second I agree to do the interview. The journalist, Mathilde Roche, is based at **Teen Me**'s European main office in Paris, but she says she can meet me anywhere, anytime, although this week would be best because they want to publish and post the up-and-coming vlogger story in next month's issue.

I figure it's okay to suggest that we meet in Waldenburg town because I'm not telling them my real name, or giving them my real address. So I could be any random person from Waldenburg, or even France (the border is only a twenty-minute train ride from Waldenburg's town centre). So I suggest to Mathilde Roche that we meet tomorrow, at the main square in Waldenburg, at 4 p.m.

She's surprised when I suggest Waldenburg and says that the location couldn't be better, because she has another interview to do in Waldenburg tomorrow, and what a surprise to have two interviews there. I'm surprised too, because who else in Waldenburg (a.k.a., Fashion Siberia) could trendy magazine **Teen Me** possibly want to interview?

We say *au revoir* and à *demain*.

I'm going to be in **Teen Me**!

I'M SO STRESSED!

I've just realized that I've broken a **MAJOR PALACE RULE**.

The palace rule clearly states: No member of the Waldenburg royal family is to have any direct contact with any journalist from **ANY** published or digital press.

My mum says it's to make sure that whatever we say to a journalist isn't misquoted, because that could cause a big misunderstanding.

So, basically, even if *Moth Collectors' Monthly* called me about a **MOTH**, I'm not supposed to contact them back, but instead direct their enquiry to the palace press office.

I can only imagine what the palace would say about me dealing directly with **Teen Me**.

Actually, I'd rather not think about what they'd say because just imagining the look Alice would give me is bad enough.

Then again, I'm not supposed to be vlogging in the first place...so basically I'm breaking all kinds of rules meaning I really am a **ROYAL REBEL!**

Outside school Max and a group from the Boys' Movement are waving posters and chanting, "We are people, too! We are people, too!"

They've clearly been waiting for me because as soon as they see me their chanting increases and they rush to follow me down the school steps.

"Where's our king?" Max asks as he faces me, his chanting followers behind him. "We've had nine hundred years of girl power – now it's time for some boy power! You, Lilian Waldenburg, need to change things. It's time you heard the people!"

"I appreciate your arguments and I'm happy to discuss your issues, but I have to get home, so if you don't mind..." I say in as friendly a manner as I can muster as I push past Max, but he insists on following me.

"Precisely: you're on your way *home* – to the palace, to see your mother, the head of our government! Perhaps at dinner you can bring up Waldenburg's problem with gender inequality?"

Max continues talking to me as I walk across

the small car park in front of the school. The rest of the school's Boys' Movement is just behind us – along with my security.

As I walk out through the school gates Max thrusts another pamphlet into my hands.

I feel I should speak with him about the whole gender inequality thing, especially now that I'm learning so much about our matriarchal queendom in Princess Class. I think that talking to Max about our long feminist history might help him understand that I can't change Waldenburg with the snap of my fingers. But he is so angry and so loud that I lose heart and instead I politely take the pamphlet and leave.

I message Leonie on my way home and she's excited about my Tiara Girl interview with **Teen Me**.

> Leonie: This is great! Just think of all the new followers this exposure might bring you!
> SO EXCITING!

Me: I know! It's WAY TOO exciting! Except I'm not sure what to say...up to now I've only ever done my Crown Princess birthday interviews, with Alice or my mum always next to me... What do you think Teen Me will ask me about? And what will I say???

Leonie: That's easy – I'll coach you! I've watched tons of celebrity interviews and know exactly what to say...

Me: Yes please!

I pass the guards outside the palace walls and push open the small iron gate that leads into the palace gardens. And even though on the outside I probably look like I do everyday...on the inside I'm a mass of contradictory thoughts.

I mean, on one hand, I'm thrilled about the publicity my **Teen Me** interview will bring Tiara Girl, but the more people who know about Tiara Girl, the higher the chance my real-life identity will be found out. So I'm basically putting everything I've worked for at risk... At the same time, however, I'm super excited because this interview is a kind of confirmation that there are people out there who are into the same kind of style and fashion as me, whatever the palace and Grandmaman and my parents may think. **HELP!**

If I were a fairy-tale princess, it would be about now that my fairy godmother would come to my rescue and smooth things out for me. But nothing like that is going to happen because this is real life, not a book or a movie, and real-life princesses don't have magical godmothers. I know this because one of my godmothers is the queen of a European country, and, as far as I know, although she is very lovely and regularly sends me silver-framed photos of herself, and extravagant gifts for my birthday and Christmas, she has no special powers. Also I don't see her that often, so she has no clue about the recent developments in my life and wouldn't know that **NOW** is the moment to step in and lend her goddaughter a helping hand.

Instead I have Alice.

And she is **SO** *not* a fairy godmother.

Chapter NINE

4 p.m., back at the palace

When I walk into the palace, Coco is there to greet me – and so is Sandra and she has a message for me.

"Princess Lily, Countess Vendelstein has asked me to let you know that she has an especially fun surprise for you tonight. She also asks that you meet her a bit earlier than planned – at a quarter to six – for your Princess Class."

This is worrying news because Alice's idea of fun, and my idea of fun, are **VERY** different. Alice's last **FUN** surprise was six months ago, just after my thirteenth birthday, when she called me into her office to give me my new monogrammed stationery.

Monogrammed stationery is many things **BUT FUN IS NOT ONE OF THEM**!

It especially wasn't **FUN** when Alice then made me write a **MOUNTAIN** – literally a **MOUNTAIN!** – of thank-you notes to everyone who had sent me letters of congratulations and gifts for my birthday. This included Waldenburgers, and all kinds of royals from around the world, as well as a few presidents and even a famous American pop star (to be honest, writing that letter actually was kind of fun).

But my birthday isn't for another six months.

So what can this mean?

I quickly saddle Cupcake, and once I've mounted we (me, Cupcake, Coco and my security) head towards the forest just outside the palace walls. I ride through the woods until I'm in the Valley of the Queens. Once there I loosen my hold on the reins and Cupcake takes off like an arrow. We gallop for a while, before slowing to a canter, then a trot, until finally we stop in a meadow. While Cupcake snatches huge mouthfuls of meadow grass, I lean backwards until my head is resting on her warm rump. I close my eyes and feel the sun on my face.

Then I look up and see the palace above us, its many turrets jutting out above the cover of the trees. The flag is flying over the largest tower of the palace – the Queen's Tower. The Waldenburg flag is divided lengthwise, into green and white, and has our family coat of arms in the middle of it: a white rearing unicorn against a red shield. I know it's my family's flag but, seriously, it's super cool! I mean how many other flags have a **UNICORN** on them?

The flag always flies over the palace when my mum is in Waldenburg – as it will when I'm queen.

I get queasy thinking about it because when that day comes it means I'll be in charge of the government and have to make big decisions for Waldenburg, which, even if it is a small country, is still nerve-racking. Also, now that I think about it, it means that I'll have a lot less time to ride and vlog and do my **DIY** projects...

But that's a long way off, thank goodness, and until then I have a lot of vlogging to do!

Alice is waiting for me when I walk into Grandmaman's sitting room for my Princess Class. "It's time for your surprise, Lily," she says as I sit down.

Alice pauses while Grandmaman passes through the room and blows me a kiss before disappearing into her bedroom.

"And I know you'll love it." Alice pauses again.

THESE PAUSES ARE KILLING ME!

"The surprise is that your favourite magazine, **Teen Me** – I know you subscribe to it – called yesterday, asking for an interview with you, and we have answered yes, on your behalf." Alice is eyeing me excitedly, and Grandmaman, who has just walked back in, is standing beside her, smiling.

"After talking it over with the press office, I accepted because I know how much you love the magazine," Grandmaman adds.

Teen Me!
TEEN ME?

Are they joking?

No, they're not.

I'm certain of this because queens and court officials never play practical jokes.

Okay.

I'm in shock.

TOTAL SHOCK.

So this is the reason Mathilde Roche, the journalist from **Teen Me**, will be in Waldenburg tomorrow: because she is interviewing me.

TWICE!

I'm the "other" Waldenburg interview she talked about!

And she doesn't know it.

How *can* she? And how can Grandmaman or Alice or the palace know?

They can't because Tiara Girl is my *secret* online persona.

I need some fresh air and head to the window, nearly stumbling on my way there.

"Lily?" asks Grandmaman as she follows me. "Are you all right?"

I see Alice and Grandmaman exchange concerned looks.

This is **SO NOT FUN**.

I gulp the cool evening air.

"Umm...yes, fine, Grandmaman. Better. I'm just so excited by this news that it's...it's...er, completely bowled me over."

It actually has. Just not from excitement.

"You don't look well, Lily. Should I call Dr Leclerc?" Alice asks my grandmother. Dr Leclerc is the head of Waldenburg town's hospital – and the royal family's personal physician.

He's also the last person I want to see right now – especially considering there is no cure for the kind of shock I'm suffering from. And as wise as Dr Leclerc is, he doesn't know what it's like to be a secret princess vlogger with a **MAJOR** problem on her hands.

"No!" I say. Only it comes out more forcefully than I want and now my grandmother and Alice are *convinced* they should call Dr Leclerc. "I feel fine, I promise," I insist as calmly as I can. "Really." Then I quickly add in a fake cough and pretend to clear my throat. "I think it's just some dust in my throat."

Alice goes to Grandmaman's bar table and pours a glass of water, which she brings back to me. I drink it slowly, dragging out the time so that I can think over what I'm going to do about tomorrow's double **Teen Me** interview.

I mean, surely Mathilde Roche, **Teen Me** interviewing supremo, will realize straight away that Tiara Girl and Crown Princess Lily are one and the same person?

Journalists have X-ray eyes. I know this from my mother and grandmother – and the palace press office. They've been telling me this since I was born.

Regardless of the risk I'm keen to do my Tiara Girl interview. I suppose I could cancel it...but it will help my vlog grow and besides it's the only thing I have that's totally mine. Like, it's different and fun to be known for being me, as opposed to Crown Princess Lilian.

But will I be able to pull this off?

Somehow I have to or I might just as well forget continuing with Tiara Girl.

And I can't let that happen…

See? Being a princess is **SO** not what it's made out to be!

I sit down and have another drink of water. Grandmaman and Alice, meanwhile, are watching me like hawks. I can't help wondering if they're onto me.

"I'm fine, I promise," I say, standing up. "And I'm super-excited about the **Teen Me** interview! I love the magazine so much!"

My **Teen Me** Tiara Girl interview is at four o'clock, and the Crown Princess one is at five o'clock, so the two interviews will be back to back.

This means I'll have to make sure my Tiara Girl interview lasts less than an hour, because I'll have to get back to the palace to change for my Crown Princess interview at five. And I can't be late, or Alice will hunt me down.

Seriously, how much pressure can a royal princess take?

I'm desperate to send Leonie a message because **I NEED A PLAN**! I can't, though, because Grandmaman and Alice are still inspecting me as if I'm a piece of porcelain from the royal collection.

But they look pleased now that I've told them that I'm excited, so at least I've convinced them for the moment that nothing is out of the ordinary.

"**Teen Me** has given the palace a list of questions which I've approved for the interview," Alice says as she takes a sheet of paper out of her folder and hands it to me. "They are all about your impending coming of age, all straightforward and rather serious – as befits a Crown Princess. You'll have to start giving more interviews as we get nearer to your birthday. That is why the palace press office and I thought that **Teen Me** would be a good place for you to start – and not just because you like the magazine. Frankly, although they mostly cover fashion and style, they also have a policy of following current events with a strong feminist/girl-power slant. You fit this angle perfectly."

"I do?"

"Of course, Lily," Grandmaman replies.

"Have you forgotten yesterday's Princess Class already?" Alice asks. She does not sound amused. "We are a queendom of independent women, a beacon of feminism and girl power. And..." Alice taps her foot.

"A proud matriarchal and matrilineal society?"

Both Alice and Grandmaman smile and nod at me.

"And we have been for over nine hundred years," Grandmaman adds. "And *you*, Lilian Athena Isabella Marie, will be the one representing all of this history and culture for the next generation."

Suddenly this *Teen Me* interview seems more like some kind of world forum or something, and I'm feeling a lot more stressed out than I was even five minutes ago.

"You are a piece of living history, Lily, don't forget!" Alice adds.

Great! As if I don't have enough to think about!

TEEN ME INTERVIEW WITH HRH CROWN PRINCESS LILIAN — LIST OF PALACE-APPROVED QUESTIONS:

1. Your official coming of age is coming up…what does this mean to you as Crown Princess of Waldenburg?
2. Are you ready to take on more royal duties?
3. What did it feel like when you realized you would one day be queen?
4. Which women leaders do you admire?
5. Which queen in Waldenburg's history do you think most highly of? Why?
6. Waldenburg is a matriarchal queendom…do you believe men should have equal rights?
7. What has it been like to grow up in a palace?
8. What are your hobbies?

"Think about your answers tonight, and we can discuss them tomorrow at breakfast. I'll be at the interview with you, so there is no need to worry about anything. Oh, the only thing I must insist upon is that you do not focus at length on your passion for fashion when you're asked about your hobbies." Alice is looking at me with one eyebrow arched.

"But I love fashion!"

"I know, Lily – the whole palace knows. But that is not the point."

"Alice is right, Lily," Grandmaman chimes in. "An interest in looking appropriate is one thing, but a passion for clothing and fashion is quite another – and something, I might add, that is not especially becoming of a Crown Princess. You must keep your mind focused on more important things, like the welfare of Waldenburg, rather than sequins and jeans."

See? I'd be knee-deep in glitter if I was given a bag of it every time I heard the word "appropriate"!

"Talk about Cupcake and Coco," Alice suggests. "Everyone knows that royal families love horses and dogs. Horses and dogs are something that everyone can relate to. High fashion isn't."

"I was going to talk about them anyway." Coco looks up at me and wags her tail when she hears her name.

"Perfect," Alice and Grandmaman say in unison.

So that's that. I'm not supposed to talk about fashion during my palace interview.

But I will be talking about fashion for my Tiara Girl interview an hour earlier.

If only Grandmaman and Alice knew!

What am I saying? Thank goodness they don't! And hopefully they never will. Can life get any more complicated than it is now? I royally hope not.

 # Chapter TEN

7 p.m., in my bedroom

> Me: Seriously, Leonie, what am I going to do? I need a plan!

> Leonie: We'll think of something… Wait! I have a brilliant idea! Think of yourself as an actor and pretend that you have two different roles to play tomorrow.

> Me: But I'm not an actor.

> Leonie: Well then you'd better decide if being a royal rebel is really your thing.

Because if it is, then you'll have to do both interviews, so you'll have to play both roles...there's no other way.

She has a point.

Me: Decision made. I'm a royal rebel and I won't give up Tiara Girl.

Leonie: Yay! I'll help you. I'll give you a call and we can start now...

I may not have a fairy godmother like a fairy-tale princess but I think Leonie is about as close to one as I can get.

We went through my entire wardrobe and sorted out my Tiara Girl outfit for tomorrow via phone. Plus we came up with a plan. A super-cool, double-identity kind of plan to get me from the first interview to the second one without being found out! I would share it with you now, only I'm tired and want to sleep, so it'll have to wait until tomorrow.

It's time for some royal zzzzzz...

So today's Thursday – the day of my double-interview challenge! I spring out of bed as soon as I remember this.

TIARA GIRL OUTFIT FOR MY TEEN ME INTERVIEW:

* My pink wig.
* My favourite jewelled headband.
* My heart-shaped sunglasses – to keep Mathilde Roche from getting a look at my eyes!
* My favourite jeans jacket with the sequinned patches, customized by *moi*.
* A super-cute pink tulle skirt I made. It goes to my knees and has three layers of tulle so it's fluffy. But just the right amount of fluffy.
* A pair of Doc Martens I've customized with paint.

My nerves are starting to get the better of me and I can't focus in class this morning.

When you have two back-to-back interviews planned with one of the biggest teen magazines in the world, it's hard to concentrate on anything, let alone Waldenburgerish verb conjugations.

Plus I swear Max is following me around again today. Every time he sees me, he and his Boys' Movement dash towards me, waving their signs in my face and chanting, "Boys are people, too!" And then Max confronts me with a long list of issues that they don't think are fair to boys and men.

But even if I do agree with him and his movement about some of the stuff (okay, maybe most of it), it's not as if I alone am responsible for nine hundred years of matriarchal history!

Meanwhile Leonie keeps giving me interview tips whenever our teachers have their backs to the class.

"Remember," she whispers during art class, "the most important thing is to give short answers that are clear and concise."

"Why?" I ask, as I draw Cupcake's pretty face, in profile.

Leonie shakes her head and sighs. "Because you have to keep things moving along so that the journalist doesn't start putting words in your mouth. Every major film star uses this tactic."

School is finally out and Leonie and I are on our way to Bergen's Department Store – the poshest department store in Waldenburg. It's six floors high and has everything from perfume and scarves to the most melt-in-your-mouth sweets. It's amazing!

But Leonie and I won't be shopping.

We'll be following my **TOP SECRET PLAN**.

MY TOP SECRET PLAN PART ONE (IN ACTION):

* Leonie and I go to Bergen's and pretend that we're looking for a new dress for Leonie's

upcoming family reunion. Good news: the saleswoman doesn't recognize me! (I'm wearing a cap and sunglasses.)

* My palace security quickly checks out the teen dress department before signalling to me that it's all safe. Then they move to the luggage and travel department, where they don't stand out as much.

* Once the saleswoman has filled Leonie's dressing room with all kinds of dresses, we both go in together. While Leonie starts to try on the dresses, I open my rucksack, take out my Tiara Girl outfit and change into that.

* When I'm ready I walk out of the dressing room and hold my breath as I calmly pass the other shoppers in the dress department and my palace security in the luggage department. I breathe a sigh of relief when they don't look twice to see if it's me underneath the heart-shaped sunglasses, customized clothes and pink wig.

* I exit Bergen's and head straight to the corner of the square where I told Mathilde Roche I'd meet her.

Mathilde Roche is waiting for me in Queen Lilian III Square. She recognizes me instantly (okay, it doesn't exactly take a journalistic genius to spot my Tiara Girl get-up) and we sit down on a bench at the edge of the square, under the shade of a large tree.

The square is named after my great-grandmother, Queen Lilian III. She was Waldenburg's longest reigning queen (79 years!) and much loved – especially by my mother, which is why I'm named after her. I remember to stop myself from blabbing all of this when Mathilde comments that it's such a pretty square.

Fortunately, Mathilde accepts my reason for withholding personal details like my real name and age. I tell her that this is so that my viewers can concentrate on my style tips and not me as a person.

She says it's a unique, but good, idea.

Then she takes her notebook out and clears her throat before asking me the first question.

Teen Me: What is your number one tip for fellow newbie vloggers?

ME: "Be yourself!" Ha! If only Mathilde Roche knew! Then again, I'm royally thankful she hasn't picked up on this.

Teen Me: We love the tiaras you make for your guinea pig, Zoë. Will you make one for your pony soon?

ME: Yes, definitely! I just have to find thick enough wire and large enough crystals. If any readers have a source to share, leave a comment on my latest video!

Teen Me: Why the heart-shaped sunglasses?

ME: Good question, Mathilde! Honestly... I just like the look.

Teen Me: So much of what you show us on your vlog you make yourself: the customized clothes, the makeover looks for you and your dog, and now the DIY in your room...where and how did you learn to do so much yourself?

ME: "I love to use my hands. And I think that adding my own personal touch to things highlights my own sense of style in a way that store-bought stuff can't. Handmade stuff has soul!"

Mathilde suddenly takes off her glasses and looks at me. "I have a final question, one I thought of on the train ride here, and I think our readers would love to know the answer... You call yourself Tiara Girl – and you always include a tiara in your videos. Why the obsession with tiaras? Have you always dreamed of being a princess?"

OMG!
SHE HAS X-RAY EYES!
SHE KNOWS WHO I AM!

I thank my lucky stars that I'm wearing sunglasses otherwise she'd see the panic in *my* eyes.

I can feel my mouth sort of hanging open and I'm at a total loss for words.

Finally the silence is broken when Mathilde says, "You wouldn't be the first girl to dream of being a princess, you know..."

The right answer finally comes to me and I say, "Actually, I think Tiara Girl is more about channelling your inner queen than being a princess. One is strong and makes decisions; the other just hangs around waiting for something to happen. So let's say the tiara symbolizes the queen in every Tiara Girl!"

Mathilde Roche puts her glasses back on, and quickly writes everything down. "Fabulous, so empowering," she says. "What great quotes! Our readers are going to love them!"

She puts her notebook away and as we stand up she says, "If you can keep a secret then I can tell you that my next appointment is with the Crown Princess of Waldenburg – in fact, I'm going to the palace right now. I think that's why I have tiaras on my mind. What a coincidence that I'm meeting both Tiara Girl *and* a princess who wears tiaras – real ones – on the same day!"

I smile and agree.

She says she'll look forward to watching Tiara Girl grow from now on. Then I wish her luck with the Crown Princess interview and leave as quickly as I can, because Alice will kill me if I'm late to the palace!

After saying goodbye to Mathilde I sneak back into Leonie's changing room (she's trying on the twentieth dress!) at Bergen's. I change back into my school uniform and quickly stuff my Tiara Girl outfit into my rucksack. Then Leonie and I leave the department store (with security behind me – they haven't noticed a thing!).

Outside we quickly hug and do the special handshake we made up for moments like this. Then Leonie wishes me good luck with my next interview before I dash back home...

♥ *Chapter* ELEVEN

4.50 p.m., at the palace

Back at the palace I rush up to my bedroom, Coco at my heels. Sandra has laid out the yellow dress I'm supposed to wear for my interview (it's plain and simple and already my fingers are itching to customize it with some embroidery). I have just enough time to quickly change into it and brush my hair.

I also let Zoë out of her cage so she can stretch her legs while I get ready (I know she has very short legs but even guinea pigs need to stretch!).

Once I've changed, I reach for the interview notes Alice has written up for me. I can still see my wig and sunglasses and the rest of my Tiara Girl interview outfit in my backpack but I don't have time to take it all out and hide it, so I stuff the notes on top of it all and sling my backpack over my shoulder.

I can't see Zoë, but I haven't got time to look for her so I decide to leave her running loose in my bedroom while I do the interview. I dash downstairs.

Alice is on the phone when I walk into the Gold Drawing Room. She's alone, so she's clearly sent the footmen out so that we'll be alone with Mathilde Roche. She waves at me.

I wave back at her but I'm not really paying attention because I'm feeling so relieved that I've made it this far without a hitch!

I'm about to punch the air with my fist when I catch sight of Alice watching me and stop midway. She has that effect on people. I don't know if it's her steely former-four-star-general stare or just her stern expression.

Probably both.

The Gold Drawing Room is well known because it opens onto the balcony that looks over the public courtyard of the palace, where the changing of the guard takes place. It's the balcony we wave from on national celebrations and my mother's birthday (which is also a national celebration – "Queen's Day" – the date changes with every queen's reign).

The room is large and the walls are covered in gold silk damask. The high ceilings are decorated with gilded plasterwork; two large crystal chandeliers catch the late afternoon light, throwing sparkles around the room. It really is a *gold* drawing room.

I sit on a sofa next to an enormous baroque chimney, decorated with an elaborately carved unicorn – the one from our family coat of arms – and pour myself a glass of apple juice from the silver drinks tray laid out on the low table in front of the sofa.

Alice has just put the phone down and tells me that Mathilde Roche will be shown in at any moment and that Grandmaman will join us as soon as she can.

As I lean back and Alice takes another call, something pink suddenly catches my eye.

HUH?

I set my juice down and rub my eyes because I think I'm seeing things.

But, no, I'm not, this is real.

OMG!

I start to panic because, at the other end of the sofa from where I'm sitting, I can see my pink wig sticking out of my backpack – and it's moving!

WHAT IS GOING ON?

I would scream except that Alice is in the room and **UNDER NO CIRCUMSTANCES** can I allow her to notice my moving pink wig or she'll start asking **WAY TOO MANY** questions!

I make a dive for my backpack, but it's too late: Alice is still on the phone, but her eyes are wide with surprise at the sight of the pink wig wriggling out of my backpack.

I reach to grab it and hear a loud squeal.

I know that squeal.

It's Zoë!

SHE'S UNDER MY WIG!

For one moment I'm actually relieved because that

means that my wig has not been taken over by the ghostly spirit of Count Eberhart. But a moment later I break out in a cold sweat as I hear Alice saying goodbye to the person on the other end of the phone and I can see she's looking around trying to find out where the squeal came from!

OMG!

Zoë must have found her way into my backpack while I was changing in my bedroom. She's done that before…but did she have to do it **TODAY**?

Zoë squeals again as I struggle to keep her from wriggling right out of my backpack.

Alice is now off the phone and heading towards me.

"What is going on? What have you done now, Lily?" she asks as she nears me. "And what is making that incredible sound?"

But just as Alice is about to reach my side, a footman walks in to announce that Grandmaman and Mathilde Roche are here. Alice immediately turns round but the commotion scares Zoë and with one last squeal she scuttles out of my backpack. In a flash she's gone – with my wig!

As Grandmaman walks in with Mathilde Roche, I stand up and catch sight of Zoë streaking across the floor. I also notice that my heart-shaped sunglasses are tangled up in the wig.

OMG! WHY DOES THIS HAVE TO HAPPEN TO ME?!

After wrestling with Zoë, my hair is messy and my dress is rumpled. I can see Grandmaman take this in as she glances at me. She is not amused. I smile lamely and try to stand so I'm blocking Zoë from their view.

"Why are you standing there like that?" Grandmaman says. "Come and meet Mathilde Roche. Lily!"

I know that tone of voice and it means there will be a lecture later. Alice's eyes, meanwhile, are practically glowing red and she's making a face that reminds me that she doesn't really need a scary costume for Halloween: she's good to go!

THIS IS THE WORST MOMENT OF MY LIFE!

"Lily, please say hello to Mathilde Roche, now," Grandmaman orders. She is looking at me sternly until I see her eyebrows go up and her eyes suddenly widen.

She's spotted Zoë!

And now Alice has, too!

OMG, OMG, OMG!
PLEASE DON'T LET MATHILDE ROCHE SEE MY PINK WIG OR MY TIARA GIRL DAYS ARE OVER!

"What is that, Lily?" Grandmaman asks me. "Did I just see something move?" I see Mathilde crane her neck to follow Grandmaman's line of vision.

"What? What are you talking about? I haven't noticed anything. Really." I jump across the room to block their line of vision. I know I must seem like the weirdest princess in the world, but what else can I do?

Grandmaman narrows her eyes at me.

I AM SO BUSTED!

Zoë has disappeared now though and for the moment everything seems normal. I take a deep breath, introduce myself to Mathilde Roche and sit on the sofa with Grandmaman, opposite Mathilde and Alice, and we proceed.

The interview starts all right, considering **MY LIFE**

IS ON THE LINE. The fact that I'm so flustered and nervous must make me seem totally different to the confident Tiara Girl of an hour ago, so that's something positive, anyway. So far, I haven't noticed Mathilde look at me with suspicion, so I'm pretty sure she hasn't guessed my secret identity. Fingers crossed things stay that way…

Mathilde Roche has stuck to the list of questions **Teen Me** sent to the palace for approval, and I have answered as per Alice's suggestions. But then, just as we're wrapping up the interview, Mathilde suddenly looks up at me from her notes and says that if she may ask one more question, she's sure that **Teen Me** readers would love to know if I, like most teens she interviews, am interested in fashion? I can feel Alice and Grandmaman watching me.

"Umm… Actually, I really enjoy walking my dog and riding my pony," I say carefully. "And, umm, some **DIY**, too."

"Oh, then I know just the vlog you should be

following," Mathilde says brightly.

I feel my mouth suddenly hang open in horror because I think I can guess what she's about to say.

CAN THIS DAY GET ANY WORSE?

Mathilde casually leans in and says, "Check out Tiara Girl. It's a super-cute vlog and I think it's really going to grow fast. I'm sure you'll love it."

I nearly explode with relief: Mathilde Roche still doesn't suspect that I'm Tiara Girl and she's just (unknowingly) praised my vlog. "Oh, thank you so much for the tip," I say. "I'll be sure to check it out."

Then I lean back on the sofa and hope this day will end as soon as possible.

My **Teen Me** interview has finished and Mathilde Roche has not suspected that I am Tiara Girl.

PHEW!

Furthermore, Zoë is still out of sight.

But we are just about to stand up when Zoë suddenly appears at my feet. She's still wearing my wig and sunglasses and is standing, her pink nose twitching, as she sniffs the air. Fortunately Mathilde Roche's head is bent over her notes and she hasn't noticed Zoë yet – but Grandmaman and Alice have. I panic and quickly reach down to pull my wig and sunglasses off of Zoë, hoping I can kick them under the sofa before Mathilde Roche sees them and makes the connection between me and Tiara Girl, but before my hand gets close enough, Zoë suddenly squeals loudly and makes a dash under the sofa's low legs.

NO, NO, NO!

Grandmaman says, "What's that?" in a very agitated voice as she looks around for a footman. Alice meanwhile reaches for her file and tries to bat Zoë with it. Without thinking I jump up and race behind the sofa just as Zoë comes scrambling out from underneath. I grab her firmly in my hands and then realize that I can't stand up or everyone will see Zoë...yet I can't just let her go and risk Mathilde Roche seeing her.

But no sooner is Zoë in my hands – still wearing my wig and sunglasses – than Mathilde Roche has twisted in her seat and is staring at me over the sofa back. I make steady eye contact and smile lamely at her while I struggle to untangle my wig and sunglasses from Zoë.

I can tell by Mathilde Roche's expression that she has never encountered a stranger interviewee, let alone such a weird princess. Grandmaman and Alice meanwhile, have noticed that I'm holding Zoë. I can just imagine the mega-lecture that I'm going to get later. But what can I do?

"Are you all right?" Mathilde Roche suddenly asks, "Can I help you?"

OMG! She cannot, **ABSOLUTELY CANNOT**, see my wig or sunglasses – or Zoë. She knows that as Tiara Girl I have a guinea pig – surely she'd recognize Zoë!

"Do you need my help?" she asks again as she peers over the sofa back.

As Leonie says, desperate situations require desperate solutions, so I go with the only thing that comes to mind. I interrupt Mathilde and say brightly, "Oh, it's nothing…just…uhmm…my pet rat." Out of the corner of my eye I watch as Grandmaman and Alice look at each other with shocked faces at this enormous lie.

Mathilde looks surprised. "You mentioned that

you like to walk your dog and ride your pony, but I didn't know you had a rat, too."

"Oh yes," I say. "But she's very, very shy and sensitive to the light!"

Alice and Grandmaman look at me as if I have lost my mind.

"It's because she's a special breed of rat, given to me by an empress – but I can't say which one," I add. "It would be indiscreet."

"A shy and light-sensitive rat? From an empress?" Mathilde pulls her notebook out again, clearly intrigued by this unusual story. "Do they really exist?"

"Yes, but they are very rare, and they are only bred in the Far East, at the empress's royal palace. And because these rats are an imperial secret, I'm afraid you cannot write about them."

Alice is nearly cross-eyed with anger and Grandmaman is clearly furious too – she's good friends with numerous empresses from the east.

I've just told the biggest lie in Waldenburg history, but what can I do…? I say goodbye to Mathilde Roche and she says she hopes I'll like her article.

Then Alice leads Mathilde out of the room and down the stairs.

"Lily, why did you lie like that? Whatever possessed you?"

Grandmaman's accusation is echoing in my ears. "Why did you tell Mathilde Roche that Zoë is a rat? She's a guinea pig, for goodness' sake. Why does it matter? And by the way, what was Zoë even doing at the interview? And what was that wig doing in your backpack? And why drag an imaginary empress into it all? The journalist will no doubt think you were talking about a real empress. I've never heard such lies in my life."

WHY?

BECAUSE! I want to scream, I had to or I risked losing my vlog – the one and only thing that is totally secret and completely mine. The one and only thing in my life that the entire palace and royal court have nothing to say about. Because if anyone like Mathilde Roche figures out that I, Crown Princess Lilian, have a fashion vlog, and leaks this story, then you and the palace will shut my vlog down, **THAT'S WHY**!

But how can I tell this to Grandmaman?

"It just happened without me meaning to say it!"

"That's not a good enough answer, Lily. And that kind of behaviour can't just 'happen'. You are a crown princess and one day you will be a queen. Your job is to represent your country with respect and dignity and truth – always."

"But I didn't mean for it to happen!" I feel bad, I really do. I've never told such a string of lies. But what else could I do?

"Then why did you?"

I don't say anything because if I tell the truth I'll lose Tiara Girl. And if I tell another lie, I'll just get into deeper water.

"When you speak, you speak for Waldenburg, Lily. If you *ever* forget that it will be the end of our nine-hundred-year-old monarchy. You were born to be a queen – and a queen you shall be. But first you must learn to be a princess."

Everything feels so unfair and I snap. "Maybe I

don't want to be a princess! Maybe I want to be like everyone else at my school! Non-royal and normal!"

Grandmaman watches me for a moment, and I start to feel nervous. Finally she says, "In that case you won't have to be a princess – at least not tomorrow night. I will inform the palace that you will not be attending the ambassadorial dinner."

WHAT?

I'd expected to be grounded.

I'd even expected to be thrown into the dungeon (by Alice).

But I didn't expect this.

What about the tiara?

What about my gown?

What about my Tiara Girl "How to wear a Tiara" video?

HOW HAVE I MANAGED TO MAKE SUCH A MESS OF THINGS?!

"But why?" I finally croak.

"Because you lied, Lily – and princesses don't lie. And because you can't expect to be a princess only when it suits you. If you are born to be a queen, then you must learn to be dutiful and to put that first – ALWAYS. Being a queen is not some kind of switch that you can turn off and on whenever you like, you know. And you must learn this now, whilst you are still a princess. One day you will have to take over from your mother, as she took over from me, and there will be no turning back for you from that point on: once a queen, always a queen."

A footman comes in to say that there is a call from the Queen of Belgium. Grandmaman says she'll take it and looks at her jewelled watch. "There will be no further discussion on this matter, Lily. I have made up my mind; you will not attend tomorrow evening's dinner. Instead, you will use the time to think about how you acted this afternoon."

TOTALLY UNFAIR!

I jump up from the sofa and, still holding Zoë, I pick up my rucksack from the floor and run out of the room.

Chapter TWELVE

7.31 a.m., Friday, in my room

Zoë is sniffing my left ear. I've taken her out of her cage and back to my bed for an early morning snuggle.

It's impossible to be angry with her for sneaking into my backpack yesterday and wearing my wig. I mean, it's not her fault. I should have made sure she was back in her cage before I left my room.

I get back out of bed and turn on my music and put a tiara on Zoë. I figure if I can't wear one today, then at least she can. I choose her pink diamond tiara.

I sit at my desk and write a short list of ideas for my next vlog, because I think I can safely say that **Tiara Girl's Top Tips for Wearing a Tiara** won't be happening.

At this point not even a fairy godmother or fire-breathing dragon could make Grandmaman change her mind about the ambassadorial dinner.

I list a few ideas, then Coco and I jump up and down on my bed, which always makes me feel better.

"Your Royal Highness?" Sandra knocks on my door as she calls from the corridor. "It's time to get ready for school."

I take Zoë's tiara off her head and put her back in her cage. Then I get dressed and Coco and I head downstairs for breakfast.

I wonder what today has in store for me. **FYI**: yes, I'm angry about the ambassadorial dinner. And not being able to wear the Queen Josephine Pink Diamond Tiara. And not wearing my ballgown, even if I didn't design it, or even customize it.

IT'S SO UNFAIR I COULD CRY!

On a more positive note, my Tiara Girl DIY secret turret vlog now has 9,227 views! I know because I quickly checked my phone on the way to breakfast.

That's **WAY, WAY** more views than any video I've ever posted before!

I'm nearing the five-digit mark!

It just goes to show that people love DIY!

Ha! Take that, everyone at the palace – see? I'm not the only one!

I wonder what will happen to the ballgown I was supposed to wear tonight. I suppose Grandmaman or Alice will suggest I wear it for my stamp portrait. That is, if I haven't been thrown into the dungeons by then.

At school after lunch, I stop to pick up some books on my way to class and make a discovery.

Someone has put a letter in my locker.

It has my name on it but I don't recognize the writing.

WEIRD!

Who could have sent it?

I'm about to open it when the bell rings, so I put it in my backpack and rush to Art.

I'm just minding my own business as I go down the

front steps of the school at the end of the day when I look to my right and see Max and his Boys' Movement. Unfortunately they notice me too, and start heading swiftly towards me, holding their signs up high. Max is yelling at me but fortunately I can't hear him clearly. I am so thankful that today is the last day of School Political Awareness Week. I really can't take any more of this.

I quickly stop to look left and right before I step off the pavement and onto the school car park, heading for the school gates opposite. Out of the corner of my eye, I notice that a boy has just come down the steps behind me and turned right. Only he is looking at his phone and doesn't notice Max and his group rushing towards him in their haste to get to me. I watch how he lifts his head and jumps to the left, out of their way – but then he trips off the pavement and into the way of a vehicle that's backing out of a parking space.

OMG!

I drop my backpack and move faster than I ever have before, covering the ground between us in what feels like two flying strides. I lunge towards him and manage to grab his jacket, pulling him onto the pavement and away from the back of the oncoming car just as we hear the squeal of its brakes. Okay, so the car was going slowly – we are in the car park, after all – but the boy is shaken. If I hadn't pulled him out of the way, he could have been knocked down.

Adrenaline is pumping through my veins, but it seems the boy is not seriously hurt – though he has twisted his ankle. The car's driver is apologizing, and Max has actually dropped his sign in his rush to reach us.

"Oh, oh, oh!" he says as he stands over the boy. Then he falls totally silent.

I know I've been stressed and everything, but Max's sudden silence at a moment like this makes me snap.

"'Oh'? You nearly caused a serious accident and all you can say is 'oh'? Yet every other time I've seen you you've had plenty to say – too much in fact. Why so quiet now?"

Max just stands there looking back and forth between me and the boy.

"Don't just stand there!" I shout. "Go and get Nurse Russell! I'll wait here with—"

"Carl," the boy says and he thanks me. His ankle is swelling quickly.

"Go on then!" I yell at Max.

He dashes into the school and comes out a moment later with Nurse Russell. Out of the corner of my eye I spot Leonie behind them.

While the nurse looks over Carl's ankle, I stand up and Max says to me, "I'm really, really sorry. My – our – intention was simply to talk to you before you left."

"Max," I say as I turn to face him, "I appreciate that you and your movement have various points you want to make, but yelling and brandishing signs as you aggressively follow me around the campus for three whole days is not the way forward. Yes, I will one day be queen. Yes, I will one day be able to change the laws (together with Parliament) and sign them into effect, but unless you are ready to discuss things in a calm and orderly fashion that does not put innocent Waldenburgers at risk, I will not be meeting you to discuss anything at all. Do you understand?"

Max is nodding his head, and looking at me as if he's finally aware that I am actually a real live human being and not just someone whose head will decorate a stamp one day. "You can call me at the palace the day that you are ready for a civilized conversation. Oh, and if you come near me with a sign once more, I will...I will..." I have no idea what I will do, so I say the only thing that pops into my mind. "I will paint glitter all over it!"

I hear some claps and cheers and I slowly realize that a small crowd has formed around us. Then Carl's father shows up and wants to thank me for pulling his son out of harm's way. Someone from the school magazine also turns up, along with a couple of journalists from local Waldenburg newspapers. They all ask for a picture and details of what happened but fortunately my security is on hand to help me deal with the journalists' questions. Considering that I had two back-to-back interviews with a journalist yesterday, and that the entire experience did **NOT** go as smoothly as planned, I say the minimum that I need to and let Nurse Russell and my security do the rest. Then I turn to leave, but as I do I feel Leonie nudge me in the ribs. I follow the direction of her gaze and spot something very surprising towards the side of the crowd.

OMG!

It's Grandmaman!

She's wearing a light-blue dress and coat ensemble today, with a matching hat. Not to mention a whopper of a brooch that nearly blinds me when I look in her direction.

And it seems she's seen the entire performance.

As if she didn't see enough of me in action yesterday.

Now she's heard me tell Max off in public.

I can hear the lecture that must be forming in her head right now about how a princess never shouts in public.

Especially her own viewpoints.

Extra-specially if they are political.

I AM BUSTED.

Again.

HOW MUCH CAN A GIRL TAKE?

I could melt into the pavement right now.

I see Grandmaman signal to her lady-in-waiting and whisper in her ear. She's probably asking her to call the palace to tell them to prepare the dungeons.

I COULD CRY!

I'm in the back seat of Grandmaman's burgundy Rolls-Royce. She has sent her lady-in-waiting back to the palace with her security so that we can sit alone – except for her driver, Werther (Officer Heinz-Walther Werther, formerly of the Queen's Mountain Cavalry, to be precise, but everyone calls him Werther), who's at this moment smoothly navigating the narrow, winding streets that lead to the main gates of the palace.

There's nothing smooth about the way I feel, though. Grandmaman has picked me up from school for a reason. It wasn't just because she happened to be in the neighbourhood cutting a ribbon. Trust me. Grandmaman only picks me up from school when she feels I need some direction. The last time was about two years ago when she heard that I'd started customizing my school skirts with a ton of safety pins (they looked amazing!). I'd fix the safety pins in different patterns and words and because I was doing it at school, in lessons, and then taking the pins out again before leaving school, I thought no one at the palace would know.

Wrong.

They found out.

So Grandmaman started taking me to school and picking me up again afterwards until I'd got the message: no customizing my school clothes.

I wish Grandmaman would just say how disappointed she is with me for having spoken my mind so loudly on the front steps of the school, so we can get this whole thing out of the way.

Finally Grandmaman speaks: "I hope you don't mind, but I wanted to meet you from school today, Lily."

HA! This *is* as bad as I'd thought.

Unfortunately Grandmaman does not elaborate – she's too busy waving at onlookers through the window. This silence is killing me! I decide that if Grandmaman isn't going to say anything, then I am.

"Grandmaman? I'm really, really sorry I got so angry on the front steps at school."

"Lily, you don't have—"

"No, I need to. I just, well, I was upset because I've been followed all week by my school's Boys' Movement—"

"But Lily—"

"Grandmaman, let me finish, please – so after Carl was nearly hit, okay, I know the car was only moving slowly but still, Max, the movement's leader, hadn't even noticed Carl in his rush to get to me, so I snapped at him! It just happened."

Grandmaman is smiling at me.

What's going on?

"But Lily, that's fine. In fact, I think you did the right thing."

"You do?"

Sometimes, like now, Grandmaman makes no sense.

Is it like this with all grandparents – or just royal ones?

"Yes, I do. I must admit that you didn't show the *composure* of a princess, however…"

HA! I knew it! I knew there was going to be some kind of catch somewhere. Here we go again: I'm still not acting like a proper princess.

"You did, nevertheless, show me something more important."

WHAT? Grandmaman is making even less sense now than she did two minutes ago.

"I did?"

"You did." Grandmaman is smiling at me again. "Far more important than showing me the composure of a princess, you showed me that you have the instinct of a *queen*. You saw a fellow citizen in need, you rushed to their aid and you firmly told the wrongdoer that he should act more responsibly. And, even better, the wrongdoer was someone who has been harassing you all week, and yet you calmly – well, relatively calmly – told him that you were open to discussion as soon as he was ready to talk in a civilized manner. Those, Lily, were the instincts of a true queen. Concern, engagement, fair action."

I'm stunned. Honestly, Werther could drive us to the moon right now and I don't think I would be any less stunned.

I look out of the window as we drive through the first watchtower and into the palace compound. Tourists line the side of the road as we drive past. Grandmaman smiles and waves through the window.

"In fact, Lily, I'm heartened to such a degree that I would be delighted if you would join us for the ambassadorial dinner tonight – unless, that is, you have a movie you'd rather watch..." Grandmaman looks at me. "Would you like to join us?"

WOULD I LIKE TO JOIN YOU?

Does the Queen of England live in Buckingham Palace?

Does Zoë love tiaras?

Is Leonie my best friend?

"**WEEEEEE!!**" I whoop with joy and Werther nearly collides with the florist's van as it leaves the palace. Good thing he's such an experienced driver and ex-cavalryman.

"Do sit calmly and wave and smile for the tourists,

please, Lily. That's enough jumping around – we're in a car, for goodness' sake."

"Do I get to wear the Queen Josephine Pink Diamond Tiara?"

Grandmaman nods as she continues to wave and smile for the tourists outside. "Yes, you do, but—"

I don't let her finish whatever it is she wants to say though because I am **SO EXCITED**!

"I GET TO WEAR THE TIARA!"

My heart is suddenly racing because this means **I ALSO GET TO DO MY VLOG AFTER ALL!** (Not that I share this news with Grandmaman.)

"Lily that is enough. Calm down."

I try to sit calmly, but I can't.

Visions of me in the purple tulle and silver sequinned dress that I designed and made dance through my mind. I'll wear it for sure in the video!

As we drive through the ornate gilded iron gates of the upper courtyard, Werther honks the car horn loudly and holds it for three seconds. This is the signal to the footmen to open the palace doors. It's used every time Grandmaman or my mum or dad drive through the gates.

The palace sentry guards stand to attention as they recognize Grandmaman's car and Werther drives us right up to the enormous second set of palace gates, which swing open as our car drives into the inner courtyard, where the public is not allowed. Two footmen are standing at the bottom of the red-carpeted marble stairs that lead up to the palace, waiting to assist Grandmaman.

I don't wait for a footman to open the car door but instead jump out by myself and run up the stairs. Then I dash into the palace and do cartwheels across the red carpet of the Guards Gallery until I come face-to-face with a pair of navy-blue pumps I recognize.

It's Alice! And once I've finished flipping back onto my feet and manage to focus on her face I can see that she is not amused.

"Hi, Alice!"

Alice rolls her eyes and heads towards my grandmother.

Grandmaman meanwhile, is unpinning her hat in front of a mirror.

"Lily," she says, as she eyes me in the reflection. I watch her smooth her hair with her hand. "However heartened I might have been to see you react the way you did at school this afternoon, I must nevertheless remind you that you are a long way from becoming a queen. In fact, as I mentioned yesterday, you must first master being a *princess*. So I suggest you begin by calming down now." She looks across to Alice. "Do you have the papers?"

Alice hands me the biographies of tonight's guests. The same papers we looked at together earlier this week – but updated with the latest confirmed guest list.

I take the file, then tell Alice I will study it while I check on Cupcake at the stables (no time to ride if I have to get ready for the dinner tonight, but I can give her a carrot!).

And before she can say anything else, I dash up the stairs to my bedroom.

I message Leonie while I walk to the stables and bring her up to date.

Leonie: FAB!

Me: I know!

Leonie: If you need my help to film tonight, I'll be on standby.

Me: Thank you!! You're the best!

Leonie: I know!!

I'm in my secret turret, preparing for tonight. The palace looks so small from up here – almost like a toy Lego castle or something. The steep roofs of the many different wings and towers are all jumbled together at varying heights and angles.

A tower falcon cries as it swoops past my window

and races towards Grandmaman's rose garden far below. I can see the last tourists leaving the palace compound as the watchtowers are shut for the day. They'll be lit up and opened later by the palace guards to let the evening's guests in.

I start taping dark paper up on the windows, so that no one below will be able to see the strong lights I'll be using later on when I film.

My mother has said that I will be allowed to leave shortly after dinner. Normally, no one is supposed to leave a dinner or reception hosted by a queen before the queen herself leaves; it goes against royal protocol. But because I'm thirteen, and the daughter of the queen hosting the dinner, I'm allowed to break this rule.

So I'll come up here and film while everyone else in the palace is still busy downstairs.

I give Coco a hug and then she follows me all the way down the long spiral staircase.

♥ Chapter THIRTEEN ☆

6 p.m., in my bedroom

I am doing some homework when Grandmaman suddenly enters my bedroom. She's holding a box and Alice is behind her.

"Here is something I think you'll be excited to try on," Grandmaman says as she hands me the small red box.

Eyes wide, I jump up and reach out for it.

Can it be what I think it is?

Alice and Grandmaman are smiling at me as I stare at them. I suddenly feel my mouth hanging open (yeah, yeah, I know, so **NOT** princess-like).

I'm so excited I can barely stand, so I sit on my bed.

The box is made of leather – and it looks old. It has brown spots and stuff, and on the corners the red leather has worn off so you can see the brown hide underneath. There are some scratches on the surface and a small gold clasp holding the lid shut.

I unlock the clasp carefully and gently open the lid. I catch my breath, because sitting on a black satin cushion is the most sparkly, dazzling, totally gorgeous tiara I have ever seen, cross my heart and hope to die.

Okay, so, yeah, my mum has gorgeous ones I've seen her wear many times, but this is different. This is the **FIRST TIME** I have held one! **EVER.** And it's so dazzling and bright that I bet if I turn the lights off, it will still **SPARKLE**.

I lift it off its satin cushion and out of the box, then turn it gently, watching as the light bounces off all of the tiny rose-pink diamonds. Up close I notice that there are many white diamonds on it, too. And some of the pink stones are stronger in colour than others.

It's a million times more gorgeous in real life than in the old pictures my mum showed me of it!

"It's beautiful, isn't it?" Grandmaman says.

"I love it, Grandmaman!" I jump up again and throw my arms around her before I start dancing around the room. "It's the prettiest most gorgeous thing I've ever seen – apart from Coco and Cupcake and Zoë. It really, truly is!" I can't stop jumping – and for once, Grandmaman doesn't try to get me to stop.

Finally, Alice says, "Princess Lily, do stop jumping, please."

"I know, it's not appropriate, is it, Alice?" I shout, as I jump. "But I can't help it!"

Alice rolls her eyes and then looks at my grandmother.

"Lily, that's enough, thank you."

"But I'm so excited!"

"You can be excited and stand still, you know," Grandmaman says.

"No I can't!"

Coco is barking now.

"Yes, you can, and you will, this instant."

"I love the tiara!" I yell as I flop down heavily on my bed again and let out a deep sigh.

"Thank you, Lily. Now, please listen: the tiara was

made for Queen Josephine II by Cartier. Josephine's mother, Queen Beatrix V, ordered it for Josephine's coming of age. Josephine was your great-great-great-grandmother, by the way. And do sit up when I'm talking to you, Lily. Thank you, that's better. Also, I've asked Jacqueline –" that's Grandmaman's personal hairdresser since, like, ancient times – "to style your hair tonight, before she styles mine. She will be here at any moment. And Alice will stay on long enough to help you place the tiara in your hair. I have to go and make a phone call or two, but I look forward to seeing you with it on later. Now stay calm and don't give Alice any bother, please, Lily."

"I never do!"

"Right. And tiaras grow on trees." Grandmaman blows me a kiss as she leaves. "I'll see you downstairs."

I flop back onto my bed as Coco licks my face and the tiara sparkles in my hands.

Jacqueline arrives and we try different hairstyles: hair down and loose, like Princess Madeleine of Sweden

sometimes wears hers. Then half up/half do\
Queen Rania of Jordan sometimes does hers; then all
up, with a high bun, and then all up with a low bun.

In the end we settle for a low bun; one that is full
and sits on the nape of my neck. It's pulled back
cleanly but still quite loose.

"It has to look soft and young," Alice keeps saying.
"The Crown Princess is thirteen, not thirty."

The hair on the top of my head is backcombed and
has more volume than I'd normally have with my hair
up, but this is because the tiara will have to rest on it.

Finally, once the correct bun shape and size is
achieved (with the help of a hair sponge in the bun),
Jacqueline pulls a few thick strands of hair loose from
the sides of my face and lets them fall. These she'll
use later. But first she very gently takes the tiara from
Alice and rests it on my head. She and Alice adjust it
until it sits just so. Alice says, "It has to be high enough
so that it rests on your head, but not so high that it
looks like a crown. Then again, it can't be so low that
nobody sees it."

Jacqueline starts to place pins all along the base of

the tiara, securing them in my hair. Then, once she's certain that the tiara won't budge, she backcombs the long loose bits on the sides and arranges them so that they sweep gently off my forehead, hiding the base of the tiara. Once she and Alice are happy with how it all looks, Alice holds a silk scarf over the tiara and Jacqueline spritzes my hair with hairspray.

FYI: hairspray is **NOT** good for jewels!

"Et voilà!" Jacqueline says as she stands back and admires her work.

And just like that I'm wearing a tiara!

YES, A TIARA!

The Queen Josephine Pink Diamond Tiara.

Life is great!

Waldenburg is great!

I'm nervous.

In twenty-two minutes precisely Sandra will fetch me and take me to the top of the Queen's Staircase – the grandest of the palace staircases. The Court Master of Ceremonies will be waiting to escort me down the stairs and into the Yellow Salon, where I'll be introduced to the new Waldenburg ambassadors.

All thirty-one of them. Plus spouses.

And various Waldenburg ministers.

In my new gown.

Which, by the way, is peach coloured and long, with elbow-length asymmetrically cut sleeves that flutter when I move. It's made of silk chiffon, with a fitted bodice and lined skirt. The lining under the long skirt of the dress has a few panels of tulle attached to it at the back, from knee height to the floor. This creates a full-looking dress "train" that trails behind me everywhere I walk. It's a real princess dress! It even sways and moves as I walk, giving the appearance that my feet don't touch the ground.

Also, hundreds of crystals (made in Waldenburg: the world's best crystal manufacturers have factories in our forests) are sewn all over it – especially on the bodice – so it sparkles almost as much as my tiara.

It's **AMAZING**!

I know Alice and Grandmaman have been preparing me for tonight but...still...even I could not have imagined how nervous I'd be as I stand at the top of the stairs, with the Court Master of Ceremonies beside me. The staircase – the very same one I often like to zip down using its polished brass handrail – suddenly seems unfamiliar to me.

Then again, I'm not used to seeing it lined with huge flower arrangements that are as tall as my dad (I'm usually in our private rooms of the palace long before all the final decoration is up), or hearing the Band of the Queen's Mountain Guards blast their horns as I arrive at the top of the stairs in a ballgown and tiara.

Nor have I ever arrived at an event by myself. (Normally I follow my mum and dad and grandmother, but royal protocol dictates that when the queen is hosting, she arrives last, so, as the second-highest ranking royal I must precede her – on my own – just as Grandmaman preceded me.)

I concentrate as hard as I can on not slipping and making a national embarrassment of myself as I descend the staircase and all eyes turn to me.

After 30 minutes in the Yellow Salon, during which time Alice introduces the new ambassadors and their spouses to my mum and me, we move to the Tapestry Hall for dinner. It turns out that the husband of the Argentinian ambassador loves fashion. For some reason Alice didn't list this detail under his and his wife's hobbies. I'm about to wave at Alice from across the table to say, "Ha! I'm not the only one here interested in fashion!" when I catch her eye and it's like she can read my mind. Her eyes suddenly flash as much as the tiara she's wearing and she purses her lips at me. I decide to keep my thoughts to myself.

Still no mess-ups – even though the third course involved eating a Waldenburg speciality: crayfish from Waldenburg Lake!

Score one for the home team!

After I correctly pull the crayfish flesh loose from the shell (okay, so the shells were pre-cracked, but, still, shellfish are always tricky!), I carefully place the discarded shell bits to the side of my plate, dip a slice of crayfish into the wild tarragon sauce and, after a few dainty bites, I've finished. I'm about to pump my fist in the air but the trumpets suddenly blast and Mum is getting up to give a speech.

I guess it's just as well.

Princesses aren't supposed to fist pump at gala dinners.

I'm back in my bedroom now – phew. The dinner went without a hitch.

I surprised everyone – myself included – by sticking to the programme and causing no chaos. At no point did Grandmaman, Alice or my mum have to give me the evil eye from across the Tapestry Hall.

Okay maybe Alice pursed her lips at me that once, but honestly, that was it.

Mum and Dad kept checking on me from across the room, and Mum made a point of including me in some of her conversations with key ambassadors.

She looked so beautiful and regal in her voluminous

red gown and famous ruby and pearl tiara, and she always knows exactly what to say. When I see her on a night like tonight, I'm not sure how I'm ever going to follow in her footsteps.

I think it's better not to think about it too much.

And my dad is so handsome and charming. I even overheard the US and Chinese ambassadors say they were thrilled to sit next to him, which is no surprise because Dad tells good jokes.

Grandmaman wore a long, light-green silk, chiffon gown with a **HUGE** diamond and emerald tiara on her perfectly coiffed, short hair. A matching brooch, chandelier earrings, necklace and bracelet completed the set (or parure – that's the fancy word for a matching set of jewellery).

Everyone glittered and the Tapestry Hall looked like a rainbow at dinner, what with so many ambassadors dressed in long colourful gowns. Their husbands, meanwhile, looked like penguins in white tie – although Grandmaman says I shouldn't say that. Apart from talking fashion with the husband of the Argentinian ambassador, I made loads of small talk about the weather, ate my dessert correctly with a fork, and Zoë made no surprise appearances – plus I made sure I set my knife and fork down on my plate while Mum gave her speech, because there were cherry tomatoes on it and I was not about to take a chance!

And now it's time for the second exciting part of the evening – filming my Tiara Girl tiara special!

Sandra comes in to help me out of my dress (you try getting in and out of a ballgown on your own!). Afterwards, in my bathrobe, I sit in a chair and she pulls the pins out of my hair. She sets the tiara down on my chest of drawers and says that my grandmother will pop by later to pick it up so she can put it in her personal safe for the night. (Tomorrow it will go to the large castle safe, with the rest of the Crown Jewels.)

As soon as Sandra leaves, I dress in my Tiara Girl outfit: the gorgeous full-skirted purple tulle dress with its sprinkling of matt silver sequins that I designed and made myself.

Then I do my make-up (glittery but light) and pack

my wig, sunglasses and tiara in my backpack. I also pack Coco's tiara – and Zoë's.

Then Coco, Zoë and I and sneak up to my turret.

As soon as I'm in my turret I turn on the lights, then stand at the mirror. After securing my wig on my head, I style it half up/half down and place the tiara on top of its loose, pink waves.

The tiara looks so cool with my pink hair! And my dress perfectly completes my look! I turn my camera video on and then step to my mark (a cross of tape on the floor). I start by talking about my dress and remember to show viewers some of the sketches I made when I designed it. I also make sure to include Coco and do a close-up of her wearing the pretty matching ribbon around her neck. Then I tell viewers how I achieved my make-up look before moving on to my hair – and the tiara!

Of course, I don't give away any details about the tiara, like where it comes from or even if it's real... I figure it looks pretty and that's enough. But I do share my tips for how to wear one correctly! I also talk them through how different hairstyles might look as I pin and unpin sections of my hair before I finish up by bringing Zoë – wearing one of her tiaras – into the frame for a close-up of us together.

It really is the best video ever!

LOVE!

TIARA GIRL'S TOP FIVE TIPS FOR WEARING A TIARA:

1. Make sure your tiara is polished and sparkly! Dull stones create a dull effect – and who wants that?

2. Always hide the base of your tiara with a ribbon – preferably a velvet one, in a colour that matches your hair. Wind the ribbon all along the length of the tiara's base. This will give your tiara a more polished look. **FYI**: it doesn't look nice to see the base of a tiara through your hair. You really just want to see the sparkly stuff on top!

3. Remember: choose a hairstyle that flatters you and your tiara.  Big tiaras need big hair. Delicate tiaras suit more natural-looking hair.

4. Use as many hairpins as you need to secure your tiara – after all you don't want it to slip! But make sure the hairpins are evenly distributed or you'll get a headache.

5. **SMILE!** Because it's not just the rocks on your head that should shine!

Filming takes longer than expected but I have some really cool stuff that I can't wait to edit! I have a pretty good idea of what I'll have to cut and trim, and there are a few bits I think would be very cute with music – like when I was trying to get Coco to sit for her close-up but instead she kept jumping off the large pink and gold armchair. And I know viewers are going to love the close-ups of my dress because I haven't filmed anything like it yet – it's a real change from my usual dungarees and jeans!

I make sure that I've saved everything on my

camera, so I can transfer it to my computer later. Then I start gathering my stuff together.

Time flies by when I'm in my secret turret and I don't realize how late it is until I look at my phone and see that it's just past 11 o'clock! I carefully put Zoë into my backpack, then call Coco, and after turning off the lights and shutting the door behind us, we carefully make our way down the stairs.

I'm scooting along the wall under the tapestry, on my way to my bedroom, Coco at my heels and Zoë in my backpack. I stick my head out from under the tapestry and look left and right – the coast is clear.

But then it hits me: the scent of roses.

That can only mean one thing.

Grandmaman!

What is she doing here?!

Suddenly I remember: Sandra had said she'd be round later to pick up the tiara!

OMG! OMG! OMG! The tiara is in my backpack!

I have to get to my room before she does!

The clicking of her heels echoes off the corridor's stone walls as she turns the corner towards my room.

She'll be here in a moment!

I dash out from under the tapestry and dive for my bedroom door. I open it as quietly as I can, tiptoe in, and shut it without making a sound. Then I quickly put Zoë in her cage, fling my backpack onto my bed and throw my hand into it, searching for the tiara. But it's jumbled up with my camera and everything else.

OMG!

I can hear her footsteps outside!

I have another idea.

While I shove my backpack underneath my bed with my foot I start pulling my Tiara Girl dress off and change as fast as I can into the pyjamas Sandra has laid out on my bed. Then I push my dress under the bed too, and turn the lights out.

I hear a soft knocking on my door just as Coco and I dive under the bed covers.

PHEW!

"Come in," I say as I sit up in my bed.

Grandmaman's tiara is sparkling in the soft light from the corridor.

"Ah! You must be tired after your long day. But wasn't it a lovely dinner? The tables looked splendid. And I particularly liked the British ambassador. It seems she and I went to the same boarding school in England. I thought you looked wonderful in the tiara, by the way, Lily. And in your dress too. I will tell your mother that I think you should definitely wear that tiara for your stamp portrait. Speaking of which, where is it? I have to put it in the safe. Sandra said she left it on the chest of drawers." Grandmaman turns towards the chest.

"Umm...actually, Grandmaman, it's in my backpack."

"Your backpack? Whatever for?"

"I thought it would be safer in there than on the chest of drawers. You know, in case someone broke into my room..."

"Lily, your imagination does get the better of you at times."

I climb out of bed and turn the lights on.

"Lily, why are you wearing your pyjama top back to front? And you still have make-up on your face..."

"I do?"

"It's as if you jumped into bed in a rush..." Grandmaman is giving me that look again – the one that makes me think she can read my mind.

"I guess I just forgot...what with all the excitement and everything."

"Hmm..." Grandmaman doesn't say more but I wouldn't bet the Crown Jewels that she believes me.

I pull my backpack out from under the bed and take the tiara out without letting Grandmaman see any of my Tiara Girl outfit. I hand it to her and she kisses me goodnight.

She's about to turn the lights out but before she steps out of my bedroom she asks, "By the way, I noticed that the tapestry on the corridor wall outside your bedroom wasn't hanging straight. In fact, one corner was stuck on the back of the chair next to it. You wouldn't happen to know why, would you, Lily?"

Oops.

I'd been in such a rush I hadn't stopped to check the tapestry after I slid out from under it. I'll have to be more careful in future.

Not that I can say this to Grandmaman.

"No..." I say instead. "Maybe it's the ghost of Count Eberhart?"

Grandmaman laughs. "Perhaps." She picks up a sketch of a dress that is lying on my night table. "This reminds me of the idea I had the other day..." Grandmaman doesn't elaborate but I can only think that she means the idea she mentioned at breakfast on Tuesday.

Instead she says, "Well, goodnight, Lily dear. I'll see you in the morning." Then she blows me a kiss and leaves.

I wonder if Grandmaman is onto me.

I wonder if she'll ever explain this idea of hers.

I don't have much time for these thoughts though, because I have to get my next Tiara Girl video ready to upload!

It's now midnight and my **Tiara Girl's Top Five Tips for Wearing a Tiara** vlog looks **AMAZING**!

And I'm not just saying that because of the Queen Josephine Pink Diamond Tiara. The whole thing looks great.

Promise, cross my heart!

Coco looks really sweet in the tiara I made her – and so does Zoë. I've added a lot of stars and some music to their close-ups. And I edited a super-cute sequence of Zoë, nose twitching, with her tiara sparkling in the lights. It's **ADORABLE!**

My pink hair looks amazing with the pink tiara. In the video I make some totally silly faces, but because I'm wearing my heart-shaped sunglasses and my pink wig, I don't feel self-conscious in the same way I would if I didn't have my Tiara Girl outfit on – so I think the silly faces actually look pretty cute! Plus the lighting Leonie showed me how to set up makes everything sparkle like, well, diamonds.

My purple tulle and sequin dress is **TOO GORGEOUS**!

Most importantly, I think my advice on how to

wear a tiara is really practical and helpful.

I click upload.

I'm too excited to sleep, so instead I go to my window and watch as the guests cross the palace courtyard and climb into their waiting cars. The guards are standing to attention and a line of lights can be seen as the cars snake their way along the curvy road from the palace towards Waldenburg town.

I know I live in the palace and that I'm a princess and everything, but still…sometimes even I have to admit that Waldenburg looks like a fairy-tale town.

Especially when Alice isn't breathing over my shoulder.

♡ Chapter FOURTEEN 😎

8.30 a.m., Saturday at the palace

Hi Tiara Girl! And welcome to your channel!

Your most recent video:

Tiara Girl's Top Five Tips for Wearing a Tiara

has had:

11,155 views

WHAT?
I CAN'T BELIEVE WHAT I'M SEEING.

I refresh my computer because 11,155 views can't
be right.

The number of views is now 11,163.

11,163!

I've reached over 10,000 views for the first time ever, and I only uploaded the video late last night!

I peer at the screen again. Most of the comments are about my purple tulle-and-sequin dress. The one I designed and made myself!

I throw my fist in the air.

DIV for ever!

I turn my music on and start dancing with Coco on my bed.

THIS IS JUST THE BEST!

After dancing for a while I get dressed. I put on a pair of riding breeches, a shirt and my favourite lilac fleece jacket because after breakfast I'm going to go on a long ride with Cupcake.

And then tonight, Leonie is coming for a sleepover.

It's basically a perfect day.

It's 5 p.m. and I'm in my bedroom waiting for Leonie. We're going to have dinner and then I'm going to help

her with her drama costume for her role in our school's performance of *Sleeping Beauty* – with Leonie playing the princess...except in our school's version of this classic fairy tale it's the prince who is cursed to sleep until woken by a kiss from a dragon-slaying princess.

Therefore, Leonie and I agree that if her character is supposed to be a dragon-slaying warrior princess then her costume needs to go up a few notches from the faded options the Drama Club has in its cupboards.

I'm also thinking that if she is going to play a princess then Leonie will need some kind of tiara, so I start making one with some heavy wire I have in my desk. Under my bed I keep a box full of beads and baubles and crystals and stuff, for all of my **DIY**. There are some very cool and rather large beads in there that might be perfect because you'd be able to see them from the very back of the school auditorium – even if Leonie's wild hair goes all springy and makes it difficult to see what's on her head.

I'm happy to have something for my hands to do because my mind is buzzing with all kinds of thoughts...

I managed to make it through my very first formal

event at the palace without a hitch. **YAY!**

My online identity is **STILL** a secret and the palace hasn't discovered that I am Tiara Girl. **PHEW!**

No one has noticed that I have a secret turret. Double **PHEW**!

I'm totally in shock and yet **SUPER**-excited by my Tiara Girl viewing figures. I mean over 12,000 views now and I only posted the video late last night!

I wonder if my vlog is going to keep growing this way. If so, I have to think up a lot more DIY projects to share with my viewers!

What about my Princess Classes? Alice and Grandmaman seem to think I need to know **EVERYTHING** about being a future queen – now. Will I still have time to vlog – even as my birthday and new official role as Crown Princess get closer?

And as my vlog grows how can I keep my Crown Princess Lilian identity a secret?

Alice and the palace must **NEVER** suspect a thing. **EVER**.

Grandmaman must not either.

Or my mum and dad.

I'm looking for a particular kind of bead for Leonie's *Sleeping Beauty* tiara. As I go around to the other side of my bed to find the box they're in, I see my backpack. It's still on the floor, half under my bed, exactly where I pushed it in haste last night, when Grandmaman walked in.

I pull it out from under my bed, unzip it and take out the rest of my Tiara Girl outfit so I can put it all away. As I empty out my backpack I find that letter that someone left in my school locker yesterday.

I'd forgotten all about it!

I rip it open at the back and unfold it.

Hi Lily,
I know that you are Tiara Girl!
But your secret is safe with me.
From,
A fan

WHAT?!
WHO CAN THIS BE?

After the emotionally charged week I've had the last thing I need right now is a **SECRET FAN**!

I feel a clammy sense of panic settle over me because, let's face it: a secret fan is also **SOMEONE WHO CAN EXPOSE MY DOUBLE IDENTITY**!

I sit on my bed, my mind whizzing with ideas about who it could be and what I can do about it. But thinking about this new twist doesn't help – it only makes me feel more nervous – so I message Leonie to tell her about the letter and she's just as surprised as I am.

Leonie: WHAT!? Who can it possibly be?

Me: I have no idea...

Leonie: Me neither. Both of us have kept Tiara Girl totally secret!

Me: I know!

> Leonie: Seriously, though, don't worry.
> We'll make a plan to deal with this later!

I stand up and flop onto my bed. I **REALLY** need a plan – **ASAP!** – to deal with this latest development. Coco licks my face as I sigh. And just when I was feeling sure no one had figured out my double identity...

Life can be royally complicated!

Leonie should arrive at any moment so when I hear a knock at my door I'm sure it's her...but it's not – it's Grandmaman. I'm at my desk writing ideas for future Tiara Girl vlog posts but quickly jump up when Grandmaman enters my bedroom. I shut my notebook and make sure to push the anonymous letter under it: the last thing I need right now is Grandmaman noticing anything to do with Tiara Girl – or asking me questions about *that* letter.

"Lily, darling, I came up to say goodbye to you now because I have a busy day tomorrow: your mother has asked me to stand in for her at some of the military exercises and parades that will be commemorating the Waldenburg War of the Alps – I'm afraid she has to be in cabinet meetings all weekend, something to do with an upcoming NATO meeting. Anyway, I'll be staying at the palace in Rosenheim tonight, but I'll be back tomorrow and then next week I have a surprise for you. I think you'll be thrilled. I'd love to tell you all about it now," Grandmaman stops to look at her tiny jewelled watch, "but I really must go. As I always tell you…"

"A princess must never be late."

"Exactly. And a queen – even an officially retired one like me – even less so." Grandmaman smiles and checks the angle of her hat in my bedroom mirror, then gives me a kiss on the cheek and a hug and turns to leave.

I briefly wonder if Grandmaman ever feels like telling the palace that she'd rather stay home and do sudoku or work in the garden (not that she ever has, but you know what I mean) instead of doing her official duties – in kind of the same way that I sometimes feel like telling the palace that I just want to vlog instead of going to Princess Class.

As Grandmaman opens my bedroom door to leave, I ask, "Grandmaman, does a queen ever get to do what she wants?"

"Hmm, that's a good question, Lily...I'd say that a queen should learn to want what her duty demands of her." Grandmaman is looking at me.

I roll my eyes and don't care if Grandmaman sees me because that's not the kind of answer I'm looking for.

"Perhaps you're thinking more along the lines of whether or not you'll be able to wear the clothes you want, or ride your horse whenever you want...that sort of thing?"

I nod.

"In that case, the answer is yes – and no." Grandmaman holds up a gloved hand when she sees me open my mouth to argue. "I completely understand that although you are Crown Princess, you are also a girl who wants to lead a normal life – I was the same. So you will have to find a balance between fulfilling

your wishes *and* fulfilling your duty, as we all do – myself and your mother included. So, for instance, when you are here, in our private rooms of the palace, I would encourage you to dress as you like and do what you like. But the second you step out of your space you must remember your role and how much it means in the big scheme of things. I'm afraid that's life, Lily – ours anyway."

I sigh.

"Don't worry – you'll learn…" Grandmaman stops and looks at me with a twinkle in her eye. "And I think the surprise I have for you next week will help…but now I really must go." Grandmaman gives me another kiss and hug then sweeps out of my bedroom, leaving the scent of roses behind her.

Now I'm **DYING** to find out what Grandmaman's surprise is!!!

When Leonie arrives a short while later we both look at the anonymous letter, but there is nothing about it that can give us any clue who wrote it.

"We have to ask around and find out who at school has been watching your vlog," Leonie suggests. Then, after a minute she says, "I know! Maybe it's Max! Maybe this is his new way of trying to get your attention?"

I shake my head. "He wants an open dialogue about gender equality for Waldenburg – so it wouldn't make sense for him to scare me anonymously."

"Good point. Hmm...maybe you'll get another letter and if you have enough of them you can go to the police and they can find out who is behind it!"

"And then the police will tell my parents everything and that will definitely be the end of Tiara Girl."

"I didn't think about that."

In the end Leonie and I decide that on Monday we'll start randomly (and carefully) asking our friends at school if there is any new fashion vlog that they've started watching. We won't mention Tiara Girl – just *fashion vlog*. And with some luck the anonymous letter writer will talk and give themselves away.

I don't know if this plan will work – but at least we have one, and I feel better knowing that Leonie is going to help me.

Then I tell her about Grandmaman's surprise.

"I bet she's going to let you design the ballgown for your stamp portrait!" Leonie says as she turns up the music and starts dancing. I have just finished making Zoë a new tiara. I take her out of her cage and try it on her. It's made with green crystals that look like emeralds. It contrasts nicely with her brown and white spots. **CUTE**!

"I hope so...although Alice told me there wouldn't be time to make one before I have my portrait taken... But maybe Grandmaman is going to insist that I can." Leonie stops dancing long enough for me to place the tiara I made for her on her head.

"It would be amazing if that happened."

"It would be the **BEST** thing **EVER**! I get excited just thinking about it!" Leonie agrees with me so we do our special handshake three times in a row with a spin between each one.

"This tiara is amazing, by the way, Lily. I love it!" Leonie is standing in front of the mirror.

I have to admit that it does look pretty cool on her.

Leonie and I start to dance again and as we do I

remember what Grandmaman told me earlier, about having fun and doing what I want when I'm in the palace. So for the rest of the night I forget all about being the Crown Princess of Waldenburg and Grandmaman's surprise and even the anonymous letter and Max and his Boys' Movement. Instead, with Leonie's help, I make lots of exciting Tiara Girl plans.

LOVE!

HOW I STARTED MY TIARA GIRL VLOG:

1. **MY VLOG NEEDED TO STAND OUT!**
   There are masses of teen lifestyle and fashion vlogs out there, but what I think makes mine different is that I always include a tiara. I sometimes wear a plastic glitter one that I won at the Waldenburg Summer Fair last year. Zoë always has one on and Coco sometimes does too. I think it's fun, plus everyone knows that my vlog is called Tiara Girl for a reason.

2. **I VLOG ABOUT WHAT I LOVE!** I wanted to vlog about something I'm passionate about and something that made me smile. For my first video Cupcake and I wore matching glitter make-up and hairstyles. It may sound weird but, honestly, it looked super cute.

3. **I TRY TO POST REGULARLY!** This can be tricky because as you can see it's very hard for me to be alone, or I have a ton of homework, or Princess Class, and so no time to film a video. But to keep my followers excited about what I'm doing, I have to post regularly.

4. **SHORTER IS BETTER!** I don't want my audience to be bored, so I try to keep things snappy or I know everyone will get the zzzzzs. I think two snappy minutes are better than five zzzz-y ones.

5. **STAYING SAFE!** Leonie made sure to tell me to stay safe online. So, like other vloggers, I never talk about where I live, or my school, or any details that people can identify me by. I know how important that is because my vlog can be viewed by anyone, anywhere (plus the palace mustn't know). And I **LOVE LOVE LOVE** being Tiara Girl!

SOME FUN FACTS ABOUT ME
AND ABOUT WALDENBURG:

My full name and title are: Her Royal Highness
Lilian Athena Isabella Marie, The Crown Princess
of Waldenburg. I have so many names because my
parents chose to follow royal tradition and pay
tribute to my queenly ancestors. It's kind of long…
so mainly the people who know me call me Lily or
Princess Lily.

1. The queendom was founded in 1073 by Queen
   Athena I and we've been here ever since.
2. They say that our palace inspired Walt Disney
   when he designed the famous Disney castle. I
   don't know if it's true, but the Waldenburg
   Chamber of Tourism would tell you it is.
3. Waldenburg has a population of 62,000 citizens.
4. Waldenburg is located so high in the mountains,
   that by law every Waldenburger has to learn to
   ski – starting in primary school. Every student

spends two hours a day skiing during winter term. That's one advantage, anyway, to living in the middle of the mountains!

5. In Waldenburg, the last Friday of May is National Sweets Day. Everything shuts down for the day and Waldenburgers of all ages dress as their favourite sweet and parade through Waldenburg's city centre. Along with Christmas, it's my favourite day of the year. My mum gives a masked ball at the palace on the Saturday after National Sweets Day.

6. Deep in our forest you'll find a huge factory that makes crystals. They produce lenses for binoculars and eye-glasses – and they make crystals used in fashion and jewellery. When I make my DIY tiaras I use Waldenburg crystals. One day I'd like to create a ballgown covered in them!

7. Our national flower is a pretty pink rose that grows wild in the mountains of Waldenburg. The rose has five petals and a yellow centre. But if you should find one

with six petals, don't pick it, but make a wish because it's considered good luck!

8. Waldenburgers love Christmas. Other countries may claim they started the tradition of the Christmas tree, but the fact is, it started here, in Waldenburg long, long ago when Waldenburg was just a small mountain village. And I'm not just saying that because I'm a Waldenburger. Okay, maybe I am. But the point is Waldenburg looks like a fairy tale at Christmas!

I hope you'll visit beautiful Waldenburg one day and see the royal palace!

Royally yours, Lily xoxo

Acknowledgements

I had such a blast writing *Royal Rebel* and creating Lily's world that I've been especially impatient to share this one with readers. Therefore I'd like to thank Usborne Publishing for joining me on this royal ride and for being as enthusiastic about discussing ponies and palaces as feminism and royal protocol. Many thanks to Rebecca Hill, Anne Finnis and Sarah Stewart for your ever-careful editing and guidance. And huge thanks to the brilliant designers Will Steele and Sarah Cronin, and to Anna Howorth and the rest of her talented gang for the stunning graphics – everything looks royally fabulous!

My wonderful agent, Jenny Savill, and the dynamic team at Andrew Nurnberg Associates each deserve a glittery tiara of thanks for their excitement and understanding in helping me get this series off the ground. Many thanks to each and every one of you!

I am also thankful to so many friends for their constant support of my writing life, but in writing *Royal Rebel* I owe a few special sparkly shout-outs. Frederik: many, many thanks for your enthusiasm and encouragement; your thoughts and insight have been a great source of inspiration. Mary, as always, your love and unfailing support have meant so much to me. Also, thank you Ellen for your heartening words, shared at precisely the moment I needed to hear them. And Gustav, as always, thank you for so much – and thank you for being you!